Books by Ernest Hemingway

THE COMPLETE SHORT STORIES

THE GARDEN OF EDEN

DATELINE: TORONTO

THE DANGEROUS SUMMER

SELECTED LETTERS

THE ENDURING HEMINGWAY

THE NICK ADAMS STORIES

ISLANDS IN THE STREAM

THE FIFTH COLUMN AND FOUR STORIES OF THE SPANISH CIVIL WAR

BY-LINE: ERNEST HEMINGWAY

A MOVEABLE FEAST

THREE NOVELS

THE SNOWS OF KILIMANJARO AND OTHER STORIES

THE HEMINGWAY READER

THE OLD MAN AND THE SEA

ACROSS THE RIVER AND INTO THE TREES

FOR WHOM THE BELL TOLLS

THE SHORT STORIES OF ERNEST HEMINGWAY

TO HAVE AND HAVE NOT

GREEN HILLS OF AFRICA

WINNER TAKE NOTHING

DEATH IN THE AFTERNOON

IN OUR TIME

A FAREWELL TO ARMS

MEN WITHOUT WOMEN

THE SUN ALSO RISES

THE TORRENTS OF SPRING

ERNEST HEMINGWAY

THE GARDEN OF EDEN

WITH A PREFACE BY
CHARLES SCRIBNER, JR.

SCRIBNER PAPERBACK FICTION
PUBLISHED BY SIMON & SCHUSTER
NEW YORK LONDON TORONTO SYDNEY TOKYO SINGAPORE

SCRIBNER PAPERBACK FICTION
Simon & Schuster Inc.
Rockefeller Center
1230 Avenue of the Americas
New York, NY 10020

First Scribner Paperback Fiction edition 1995

SCRIBNER PAPERBACK FICTION and design are trademarks of Macmillan Library Reference USA, Inc. under license by Simon & Schuster, the publisher of this work.

Manufactured in the United States of America

10

Library of Congress Cataloging-in-Publication Data
Hemingway, Ernest, 1899–1961.
The Garden of Eden / Ernest Hemingway; with a preface by
Charles Scribner, Jr.—1st Scribner Paperback Fiction ed.
p. cm.
1. Man-woman relationship—France—Riviera—Fiction.
2. Married people—France—Riviera—Fiction. I. Title.
PS3515.E37G37 1995
813'.52—dc20
95-15326
CIP

ISBN 0-684-80452-2

Publisher's Note

As was also the case with Hemingway's earlier posthumous work *Islands in the Stream,* this novel was not in finished form at the time of the author's death. In preparing the book for publication we have made some cuts in the manuscript and some routine copy editing corrections. Beyond a very small number of minor interpolations for clarity and consistency, nothing has been added. In every significant respect the work is all the author's.

Preface

by Charles Scribner, Jr.

UP TO THE TIME of his death in 1961 Ernest Hemingway was working on a number of writing projects, all of which were near enough to completion to be edited and published posthumously. I remember his widow, Mary, coming to my office with a large shopping bag filled almost to bursting with photocopies of unpublished writing left by her husband. This may have been one of the richest collections of literary material ever delivered in so informal a manner. In addition to a number of sketches and fragments of stories and some completed stories, the bag contained the typescripts of three major works: a novel set in Bimini and Cuba, later published under the title *Islands in the Stream,* the original transcript of Hemingway's bullfighting journal, *The Dangerous Summer,* and a major work of fiction to which Hemingway had given the title *The Garden of Eden.*

This last work was filled with so many remarkable riches that, in spite of the fact that Hemingway never completed it, we were convinced that it should be published. Only the second part was incomplete, and the first half taken by itself, with only a modest amount of pruning, provided a wholly harmonious and coherent narrative.

Upon publication of the novel, our judgment in bringing out the book as we did was confirmed by its success all over the world and by the many positive responses of leading critics.

For many readers familiar with Hemingway's other works, *The Garden of Eden* may seem to be a departure from his usual themes, in so far as it presents an intensive study of the mental state of an intelligent woman uncontrollably envious of her husband's success as a writer and yearning to change her gender.

But the conception of Hemingway as a writer primarily absorbed with external action fails to take into account his profound interest in character. On the surface, many of his stories may seem to deal with exciting physical events, but, like Conrad, he was always primarily interested in the effect such events had in the minds of the individuals concerned. As a writer he was a gifted student of human behavior. Mary Hemingway once told me that he had the uncanny knack of being able to enter a room full of people and almost immediately divine the relationships among them.

In almost all of his stories, from the earliest ones that deal with his boyhood to the great later works of fiction, one can always find the interplay of character under the surface of the action. His brief character studies in *A Moveable Feast* are additional instances of that preoccupation.

I remember his annoyance when I once suggested to him that it might be useful to teachers if we published an edition of *The Old Man and the Sea* with the original version that had appeared as a short story in *Esquire* many years before. For some time I wondered about his reaction until I finally realized that for Hemingway every story had an inside and an outside. The outside might be the basis for a good yarn, as it was in the *Esquire* short story, but only its inside, revealed by the thoughts of the old man in the final novella, could be the basis for a work of literature.

In *The Garden of Eden*, the careful reader will find such delights and revelations.

BOOK ONE

Chapter One

THEY WERE LIVING at le Grau du Roi then and the hotel was on a canal that ran from the walled city of Aigues Mortes straight down to the sea. They could see the towers of Aigues Mortes across the low plain of the Camargue and they rode there on their bicycles at some time of nearly every day along the white road that bordered the canal. In the evenings and the mornings when there was a rising tide sea bass would come into it and they would see the mullet jumping wildly to escape from the bass and watch the swelling bulge of the water as the bass attacked.

A jetty ran out into the blue and pleasant sea and they fished from the jetty and swam on the beach and each day helped the fishermen haul in the long net that brought the fish up onto the long sloping beach. They drank aperitifs in the cafe on the corner facing the sea and watched the sails of the mackerel fishing boats out in the Gulf of Lions. It was late in the spring and the mackerel were running and fishing people of the port were very busy. It was a cheerful and friendly town and the young couple liked the hotel, which had four rooms upstairs and a restaurant and two billiard tables downstairs facing the canal and the light-house. The room they lived in looked like the painting of Van Gogh's room at Arles except there was a double bed and two big windows and you could look out across the water and the marsh and sea meadows to the white town and bright beach of Palavas.

They were always hungry but they ate very well. They were hungry for breakfast which they ate at the cafe, ordering brioche and café au lait and eggs, and the type of preserve that they chose and the manner in which the eggs were to be cooked was an excitement. They were always so hungry for breakfast that the girl often had a headache until the coffee came. But the coffee took the headache away. She took her coffee without sugar and the young man was learning to remember that.

On this morning there was brioche and red raspberry pre-serve and the eggs were boiled and there was a pat of butter that melted as they stirred them and salted them lightly and ground pepper over them in the cups. They were big eggs and fresh and the girl's were not cooked quite as long as the young man's. He remembered that easily and he was happy with his which he diced up with the spoon and ate with only the flow of the butter to moisten them and the fresh early morning texture and the bite of the coarsely ground pepper grains and the hot coffee and the chickory-fragrant bowl of café au lait.

The fishing boats were well out. They had gone out in the dark with the first rising of the breeze and the young man and the girl had wakened and heard them and then curled together under the sheet of the bed and slept again. They had made love when they were half awake with the light bright outside but the room still shadowed and then had lain together and been happy and tired and then made love again. Then they were so hungry that they did not think they would live until breakfast and now they were in the cafe eating and watching the sea and the sails and it was a new day again.

"What are you thinking?" the girl asked.

"Nothing."

"You have to think something."

"I was just feeling."

"How?"

"Happy."

"But I get so hungry," she said. "Is it normal do you think? Do you always get so hungry when you make love?"

"When you love somebody."

"Oh, you know too much about it," she said.

"No."

"I don't care. I love it and we don't have to worry about anything do we?"

"Nothing."

"What do you think we should do?"

"I don't know," he said. "What do you?"

"I don't care at all. If you'd like to fish I should write a letter or maybe two and then we could swim before lunch."

"To be hungry?"

"Don't say it. I'm getting hungry already and we haven't finished breakfast."

"We can think about lunch."

"And then after lunch?"

"We'll take a nap like good children."

"That's an absolutely new idea," she said. "Why have we never thought of that?"

"I have these flashes of intuition," he said. "I'm the inventive type."

"I'm the destructive type," she said. "And I'm going to destroy you. They'll put a plaque up on the wall of the building outside the room. I'm going to wake up in the night and do something to you that you've never even heard of or imagined. I was going to last night but I was too sleepy."

"You're too sleepy to be dangerous."

"Don't lull yourself into any false security. Oh darling let's have it hurry up and be lunch time."

They sat there in their striped fishermen's shirts and the shorts they had bought in the store that sold marine supplies, and they were very tan and their hair was streaked and faded by the sun and the sea. Most people thought they were brother and sister until they said they were married. Some did not believe that they were married and that pleased the girl very much.

In those years only a very few people had ever come to the Mediterranean in the summer time and no one came to le Grau du Roi except a few people from Nîmes. There was no casino and no entertainment and except in the hottest months when people came to swim there was no one at the hotel. People did not wear fishermen's shirts then and this girl that he was married to was the first girl he had ever seen wearing one. She had bought the shirts for them and then had washed them in the basin in their room at the hotel to take the stiffness out of them. They were stiff and built for hard wear but the washings softened them and now they were worn and softened enough so that when he looked at the girl now her breasts showed beautifully against the worn cloth.

No one wore shorts either around the village and the girl could not wear them when they rode their bicycles. But in the village it did not matter because the people were very friendly and only the local priest disapproved. But the girl went to mass on Sunday wearing a skirt and a long-sleeved cashmere sweater with her hair covered with a scarf and the young man stood in the back of the church with the men. They gave twenty francs which was more than a dollar then and since the priest took up the collection himself their attitude toward the church was known and the wearing of shorts in the village was regarded as an eccentricity by foreigners rather than an attempt against the morality of the ports of the Camargue. The priest did not speak to them when they wore shorts but he did not denounce them and when they wore trousers in the evening the three of them bowed to each other.

"I'll go up and write the letters," the girl said and she got up and smiled at the waiter and went out of the cafe.

"Monsieur is going to fish?" the waiter asked when the young man, whose name was David Bourne, called him over and paid him.

"I think so. How is the tide?"

"This tide is very good," the waiter said. "I have some bait if you want it."

"I can get some along the road."

"No. Use this. They're sandworms and there are plenty."

"Can you come out?"

"I'm on duty now. But maybe I can come out and see how you do. You have your gear?"

"It's at the hotel."

"Stop by for the worms."

At the hotel the young man wanted to go up to the room and see the girl but instead he found the long, jointed bamboo pole and the basket with his fishing gear behind the desk where the room keys hung and went back out into the brightness of the road and on down to the cafe and out onto the glare of the jetty. The sun was hot but there was a fresh breeze and the tide was just starting to ebb. He wished that he had brought a casting rod and spoons so that he might cast out across the flow of the water from the canal over the rocks on the far side but instead he rigged his long pole with its cork and quill float and let a sandworm float gently along at a depth where he thought fish might be feeding.

He fished for some time with no luck and watched the mackerel boats tacking back and forth out on the blue sea and the shadows the high clouds made on the water. Then his float went under in a sharp descent with the line angling stiffly and he brought the pole up against the pull of a fish that was strong and driving wildly and making the line hiss through the water. He tried to hold it as lightly as he could and the long pole was bent to the breaking point of the line and trace by the fish which kept trying to go toward the open sea. The young man walked with him on the jetty to ease the strain but the fish kept pulling so that as he drove a quarter of the rod was forced under water.

The waiter had come from the cafe and was very excited. He was talking by the young man's side saying, "Hold him. Hold him. Hold him as softly as you can. He'll have to tire. Don't let him break. Soft with him. Softly. Softly."

There was no way the young man could be softer with him except to get into the water with the fish and that did not make sense as the canal was deep. If I could only walk along the bank with him, he thought. But they had come to the very end of the jetty. More than half the pole was under water now.

"Just hold him softly," the waiter pleaded. "It's a strong trace."

The fish bored deep, ran, zig-zagged and the long bamboo pole bent with his weight and his rapid, driving strength. Then he came up thrashing at the surface and then was down again and the young man found that although the fish felt as strong as ever the tragic violence was lessened and now he could be led around the end of the jetty and up the canal.

"Softly does it," the waiter said. "Oh softly now. Softly for us all."

Twice more the fish forced his way out to the open sea and twice the young man led him back and now he was leading him gently along the jetty toward the cafe.

"How is he?" asked the waiter.

"He's fine but we've beaten him."

"Don't say it," the waiter said. "Don't say it. We must tire him. Tire him. Tire him."

"He's got my arm tired," the young man said.

"Do you want me to take him?" the waiter asked hopefully.

"My God no."

"Just easy, easy, easy. Softly, softly, softly," the waiter said.

The young man worked the fish past the terrace of the cafe and into the canal. He was swimming just under the surface but was still strong and the young man wondered if they would take him all the way up the canal through the length of the town. There were many other people now and as they went by the hotel the girl saw them out of the window and shouted, "Oh what a wonderful fish! Wait for me! Wait for me!"

She had seen the fish clearly from above and his length and the shine of him in the water and her husband with the bamboo pole bent almost double and the procession of people following. When she got down to the canal bank and, running, caught up with the people, the procession had stopped. The waiter was in the water at the edge of the canal and her husband was guiding the fish slowly against the bank where there was a clump of weeds growing. The fish was on the surface now and the waiter bent down and brought his hands together from either side and then lifted the fish with his thumbs in both his gills and moved up the bank of the canal with him. He was a heavy fish and the waiter held him high against his chest with the head under his chin and the tail flopping against his thighs.

Several men were pounding the young man on the back and putting their arms around him and a woman from the fish market kissed him. Then the girl had her arms around him and kissed him and he said, "Did you see him?"

Then they all went over to see him laid out on the side of the road silver as a salmon and dark gunmetal shining on his back. He was a handsome beautifully built fish with great live eyes and he breathed slowly and brokenly.

"What is he?"

"A *loup*," he said. "That's a sea bass. They call them *bar* too. They're a wonderful fish. This is the biggest one I've ever seen."

The waiter, whose name was André, came over and put his arms around David and kissed him and then he kissed the girl.

"Madame, it is necessary," he said. "It is truly necessary. No one ever caught such a fish on such tackle."

"We better have him weighed," David said.

They were at the cafe now. The young man had put the tackle away, after the weighing, and washed up and the fish was on a block of ice that had come in the *camion* from Nîmes to ice the mackerel catch. The fish had weighed a little over fifteen pounds. On the ice he was still silver and beautiful but the color on his back had changed to gray. Only his eyes still looked alive. The mackerel fishing boats were coming in now and the women were unloading the shining blue and green and silver mackerel from the boats into baskets and carrying the heavy baskets on their heads to the fish house. It was a very good catch and the town was busy and happy.

"What are we going to do with the big fish?" the girl asked.

"They're going to take him in and sell him," the young man said. "He's too big to cook here and they say it would be wicked to cut him up. Maybe he'll go right up to Paris. He'll end in some big restaurant. Or somebody very rich will buy him."

"He was so beautiful in the water," she said. "And when André held him up. I couldn't believe him when I saw him out of the window and you with your mob following you."

"We'll get a small one for us to eat. They're really wonderful. A small one ought to be grilled with butter and with herbs. They're like striped bass at home."

"I'm excited about the fish," she said. "Don't we have wonderful simple fun?"

They were hungry for lunch and the bottle of white wine was cold and they drank it as they ate the celery *rémoulade* and the small radishes and the home pickled mushrooms from the big glass jar. The bass was grilled and the grill marks showed on the silver skin and the butter melted on the hot plate. There was sliced lemon to press on the bass and fresh bread from the bakery and the wine cooled their tongues of the heat of the fried potatoes. It was good light, dry, cheerful unknown white wine and the restaurant was proud of it.

"We're not great conversationalists at meals," the girl said. "Do I bore you, darling?"

The young man laughed.

"Don't laugh at me, David."

"I wasn't. No. You don't bore me. I'd be happy looking at you if you never said a word."

He poured her another small glass of the wine and filled his own.

"I have a big surprise. I didn't tell you, did I?" the girl said.

"What sort of surprise?"

"Oh it's very simple but it's very complicated."

"Tell me."

"No. You might like it and maybe you couldn't stand it."

"It sounds too dangerous."

"It's dangerous," she said. "But don't ask me. I'm going up to the room if I may."

The young man paid for the lunch and drank the wine that was left in the bottle. Then he went upstairs. The girl's clothes were folded on one of the Van Gogh chairs and she was waiting for him in the bed with the sheet over her. Her hair was spread out over the pillow and her eyes were laughing and he lifted the sheet and she said, "Hello, darling. Did you have a nice lunch?"

Afterwards they lay together with his arm under her head and were happy and lazy and he felt her turn her head from side to side and stroke it against his cheek. It felt silky and barely roughened from the sun and the sea. Then with her hair all forward over her face so it touched him as her head moved she started to play with him lightly and exploringly and then with delight and she said, "You do love me, don't you?"

He nodded and kissed the top of her head and then turned her head and held it and kissed her lips.

"Oh," she said. "Oh."

A long time later they were lying each holding the other close and she said, "And you love me just the way I am? You're sure."

"Yes," he said. "So much yes."

"Because I'm going to be changed."

"No," he said. "No. Not changed."

"I'm going to," she said. "It's for you. It's for me too. I won't pretend it's not. But it will do something to you. I'm sure but I shouldn't say it."

"I like surprises but I like everything the way it is just now at this minute."

"Then maybe I shouldn't do it," she said. "Oh I'm sad. It was such a wonderful dangerous surprise. I thought about it for days and I didn't decide until this morning."

"If it's something you really want."

"It is," she said. "And I'm going to do it. You've liked everything we've done so far haven't you?"

"Yes."

"All right."

She slipped out of bed and stood straight with her long brown legs and her beautiful body tanned evenly from the far beach where they swam without suits. She held her shoulders back and her chin up and she shook her head so her heavy tawny hair slapped around her cheeks and then bowed forward so it all fell forward and covered her face. She pulled the striped shirt over her head and then shook her hair back and then sat in the chair in front of the mirror on the dresser and brushed it back looking at it critically. It fell to the top of her shoulders. She shook her head at the mirror. Then she pulled on her slacks and belted them and put on her faded blue rope-soled shoes.

"I have to ride up to Aigues Mortes," she said.

"Good," he said. "I'll come too."

"No. I have to go alone. It's about the surprise."

She kissed him goodbye and went down and he watched her mount her bicycle and go up the road riding smoothly and easily, her hair blowing in the wind.

The afternoon sun was in the window now and the room was too warm. The young man washed and put on his clothes and went down to walk on the beach. He knew he should swim but he was tired and after he had walked along the beach and then along a path through the salt grass that led inland for a way he went back along the beach to the port and climbed up to the cafe. In the cafe he found the paper and ordered himself a *fine à l'eau* because he felt empty and hollow from making love.

They had been married three weeks and had come down on the train from Paris to Avignon with their bicycles, a suitcase with their town clothes, and a rucksack and a musette bag. They stayed at a good hotel in Avignon and left the suitcase there and had thought that they would ride to the Pont du Gard. But the mistral was blowing so they rode with the mistral down to Nîmes and stayed there at the Imperator and then had ridden down to Aigues Mortes still with the heavy wind behind them and then on to le Grau du Roi. They had been there ever since.

It had been wonderful and they had been truly happy and he had not known that you could love anyone so much that you cared about nothing else and other things seemed inexistent. He had many problems when he married but he had thought of none of them here nor of writing nor of anything but being with this girl whom he loved and was married to and he did not have the sudden deadly clarity that had always come after intercourse.

That was gone. Now when they had made love they would eat and drink and make love again. It was a very simple world and he had never been truly happy in any other. He thought that it must be the same with her and certainly she acted in that way but today there had been this thing about the change and the surprise. But maybe it would be a happy change and a good surprise. The brandy and water as he drank it and read the local paper made him look forward to whatever it was.

This was the first time since they had come on the wedding trip that he had taken a drink of brandy or whiskey when they were not together. But he was not working and his only rules about drinking were never to drink before or while he was working. It would be good to work again but that would come soon enough as he well knew and he must remember to be unselfish about it and make it as clear as he could that the enforced loneliness was regrettable and that he was not proud of it. He was sure she would be fine about it and she had her own resources but he hated to think of it, the work, starting when they were as they were now. It never could start of course without the clarity and he wondered if she knew that and if that was why she drove beyond what they had for something new that nothing could break. But what could it be? They could not be held tighter together than they were now and there was no badness afterwards. There was only happiness and loving each other and then hunger and replenishing and starting over.

He found that he had drunk the *fine à l'eau* and that it was getting late in the afternoon. He ordered another and started to concentrate on the paper. But the paper did not interest him as it should and he was looking out at the sea with late afternoon sun heavy on it when he heard her come into the cafe and say in her throaty voice, "Hello darling."

She came quickly to the table and sat down and lifted her chin and looked at him with the laughing eyes and the golden face with the tiny freckles. Her hair was cropped as short as a boy's. It was cut with no compromises. It was brushed back, heavy as always, but the sides were cut short and the ears that grew close to her head were clear and the tawny line of her hair was cropped close to her head and smooth and sweeping back. She turned her head and lifted her breasts and said, "Kiss me please."

He kissed her and looked at her face and at her hair and he kissed her again.

"Do you like it? Feel it how smooth. Feel it in back," she said. He felt it in back.

"Feel on my cheek and feel in front of my ear. Run your fingers up at the sides.

"You see," she said. "That's the surprise. I'm a girl. But now I'm a boy too and I can do anything and anything and anything."

"Sit here by me," he said. "What do you want, brother."

"Oh thank you," she said. "I'll take what you're having. You see why it's dangerous, don't you?"

"Yes. I see."

"But wasn't I good to do it?"

"Maybe."

"Not maybe. No. I thought about it. I've thought all about it. Why do we have to go by everyone else's rules? We're us."

"We were having a good time and I didn't feel any rules."

"Would you please just put your hand over it again."

He did and he kissed her.

"Oh you're sweet," she said. "And you do like it. I can feel and I can tell. You don't have to love it. Just like it at first."

"I like it," he said. "And you have such a beautifully shaped head that it is very beautiful with the lovely bones of your face."

"Don't you like it at the sides?" she asked. "It isn't faked or phony. It's a true boy's haircut and not from any beauty shop."

"Who cut it?"

"The coiffeur at Aigues Mortes. The one who cut your hair a week ago. You told him how you wanted yours cut then and

I told him to cut mine just the same as yours. He was very nice and wasn't at all surprised. He wasn't worried at all. He said exactly like yours? And I said exactly. Doesn't it do anything to you, David?"

"Yes," he said.

"Stupid people will think it is strange. But we must be proud. I love to be proud."

"So do I," he said. "We'll start being proud now."

They sat there in the cafe and watched the reflection of the setting sun over the water and watched the dusk come to the town and they drank the *fine à l'eau*. People came by the cafe without being rude to see the girl because they had been the only foreigners in the village and had been there now nearly three weeks and she was a great beauty and they liked her. Then there had been the big fish today and ordinarily there would have been much talk about that but this other was a big thing in the village too. No decent girls had ever had their hair cut short like that in this part of the country and even in Paris it was rare and strange and could be beautiful or could be very bad. It could mean too much or it could only mean showing the beautiful shape of a head that could never be shown as well.

They ate a steak for dinner, rare, with mashed potatoes and flageolets and a salad and the girl asked if they might drink Tavel. "It is a great wine for people that are in love," she said.

She had always looked, he thought, exactly her age which was now twenty-one. He had been very proud of her for that. But tonight she did not look it. The lines of her cheekbones showed clear as he had never seen them before and she smiled and her face was heartbreaking.

In the room it was dark with only a little light from outside. It was cool now with the breeze and the top sheet was gone from the bed.

"Dave, you don't mind if we've gone to the devil, do you?"

"No, girl," he said.

"Don't call me girl."

"Where I'm holding you you are a girl," he said. He held her tight around her breasts and he opened and closed his fingers feeling her and the hard erect freshness between his fingers.

"They're just my dowry," she said. "The new is my surprise. Feel. No leave them. They'll be there. Feel my cheeks and the back of my neck. Oh it feels so wonderful and good and clean and new. Please love me David the way I am. Please understand and love me."

He had shut his eyes and he could feel the long light weight of her on him and her breasts pressing against him and her lips on his. He lay there and felt something and then her hand holding him and searching lower and he helped with his hands and then lay back in the dark and did not think at all and only felt the weight and the strangeness inside and she said, "Now you can't tell who is who can you?"

"No."

"You are changing," she said. "Oh you are. You are. Yes you are and you're my girl Catherine. Will you change and be my girl and let me take you?"

"You're Catherine."

"No. I'm Peter. You're my wonderful Catherine. You're my beautiful lovely Catherine. You were so good to change. Oh thank you, Catherine, so much. Please understand. Please know and understand. I'm going to make love to you forever."

At the end they were both dead and empty but it was not over. They lay side by side in the dark with their legs touching and her head was on his arm. The moon had risen and there was a little more light in the room. She ran her hand exploringly down over his belly without looking and said, "You don't think I'm wicked?"

"Of course not. But how long have you thought about that?"

"Not all the time. But quite a lot. You were so wonderful to let it happen."

The young man put his arms around the girl and held her very tight to him and felt her lovely breasts against his chest and kissed her on her dear mouth. He held her close and hard and inside himself he said goodbye and then goodbye and goodbye.

"Let's lie very still and quiet and hold each other and not think at all," he said and his heart said goodbye Catherine goodbye my lovely girl goodbye and good luck and goodbye.

Chapter Two

HE STOOD UP and looked up and down the beach, corked the bottle of oil and put it in a side pocket of the rucksack and then walked down to the sea feeling the sand grow cool under his feet. He looked at the girl on her back on the sloping beach, her eyes closed, her arms against her sides, and behind her the slanted square of canvas and the first tufts of beach grass. She ought not to stay too long in that position with the sun straight up and down on her, he thought. Then he walked out and dove flat into the clear cold water and turned on his back and swam backstroke out to sea watching the beach beyond the steady beat of his legs and feet. He turned in the water and swam down to the bottom and touched the coarse sand and felt the heavy ridges of it and then came up to the surface and swam steadily in, seeing how slow he could keep the beat of his crawl. He walked up to the girl and saw that she was asleep. He found his wristwatch in the rucksack to check the time when he should wake her. There was a cold bottle of white wine wrapped in a newspaper and with their towels around it. He uncorked it without removing the paper or the towels and took a cool draught from the awkward bundle. Then he sat down to watch the girl and to look out to sea.

This sea was always colder than it looked, he thought. It did not really warm until the middle of summer except on the shallow beaches. This beach dropped off quite suddenly and the water had been sharply cold until the swimming warmed him. He looked out at the sea and the high clouds and noticed how far the fishing fleet was working to the westward. Then he looked at the girl sleeping on the sand that was quite dry now and beginning to blow delicately with the rising wind when his feet stirred.

During the night he had felt her hands touching him. And when he woke it was in the moonlight and she had made the dark magic of the change again and he did not say no when she spoke to him and asked the questions and he felt the change so that it hurt him all through and when it was finished after they were both exhausted she was shaking and she whispered to him, "Now we have done it. Now we really have done it."

Yes, he thought. Now we have really done it. And when she went to sleep suddenly like a tired young girl and lay beside him lovely in the moonlight that showed the beautiful new strange line of her head as she slept on her side he leaned over and said to her but not aloud, "I'm with you. No matter what else you have in your head I'm with you and I love you."

In the morning he had been very hungry for breakfast but he waited for her to wake. He kissed her finally and she woke and smiled and got up sleepily and washed in the big basin and slouched in front of the mirror of the armoire and brushed her hair and looked at the mirror unsmiling and then smiled and touched her cheeks with the tips of her fingers and pulled a striped shirt over her head and then kissed him. She stood straight so her breasts pushed against his chest and she said, "Don't worry, David. I'm your good girl come back again."

But he was very worried now and he thought what will become of us if things have gone this wildly and this dangerously and this fast? What can there be that will not burn out in a fire that rages like that? We were happy and I am sure she was happy. But who ever knows? And who are you to judge and who participated and who accepted the change and lived it? If that is what she wants who are you not to wish her to have it? You're lucky to have a wife like her and a sin is what you feel bad after and you don't feel bad. Not with the wine you don't feel bad, he told himself, and what will you drink when the wine won't cover for you?

He took the bottle of oil out of the rucksack and put a little oil on the girl's chin and on her cheeks and on her nose and found a blue faded patterned handkerchief in the canvas pocket of the rucksack and laid it across her breast.

"Must I stop?" the girl asked. "I'm having the most wonderful dream."

"Finish the dream," he said.

"Thank you."

In a few minutes she breathed very deeply and shook her head and sat up.

"Let's go in now," she said.

They went in together and swam out and then played under water like porpoises. When they swam in they dried each other off with towels and he handed her the bottle of wine that was still cool in the rolled newspaper and they each took a drink and she looked at him and laughed.

"It's nice to drink it for thirst," she said. "You don't really mind being brothers do you?"

"No." He touched her forehead and her nose and then her

cheeks and chin with the oil and then put it carefully above and behind her ears.

"I want to get behind my ears and neck tanned and over my cheekbones. All the new places."

"You're awfully dark, brother," he said. "You don't know how dark."

"I like it," the girl said. "But I want to be darker."

They lay on the beach on the firm sand that was dry now but still cool after the high tide had fallen. The young man put some oil on the palm of his hand and spread it lightly with his fingers over the girl's thighs and they glowed warm as the skin took the oil. He went on spreading it over her belly and breasts and the girl said sleepily, "We don't look very much like brothers when we're this way do we?"

"No."

"I'm trying to be such a very good girl," she said. "Truly you don't have to worry darling until night. We won't let the night things come in the day."

At the hotel the postman was having a drink while he waited for the girl to sign for a large forwarding envelope heavy with enclosed letters from her bank in Paris. There were three letters re-addressed from his bank, too. It was the first mail since they had sent the hotel as a forwarding address. The young man gave the postman five francs and asked him to have another glass of wine with him at the zinc bar. The girl unhooked the key from the board and said, "I'll go up to the room and get cleaned up and meet you at the cafe."

After he finished his glass he said goodbye to the postman and walked down along the canal to the cafe. It was good to sit in the shade after walking back bareheaded in the sun from the far beach and it was pleasant and cool in the cafe. He ordered a vermouth and soda and took out his pocket knife and slit open his letters. All three envelopes were from his publishers and two of them were fat with clippings and the proofs of advertisements. He glanced at the clippings and then read the long letter. It was cheerful and guardedly optimistic. It was too early to tell how the book would do but everything looked good. Most of the reviews were excellent. Of course there were some. But that was to be expected. Sentences had been underlined in the reviews that would probably be used in the future advertisements. His publisher wished he could say more about how the book would do but he never made predictions as to sales. It was bad practice. The point was that the book could not have been better received. The reception was sensational really. But he would see the clippings. The first printing had been five thousand copies and on the strength of the reviews a second printing had been ordered. The upcoming advertisements would carry the phrase *Now in Its Second Printing*. His publisher hoped that he was as happy as he deserved to be and taking the rest that he so richly deserved. He sent his best greetings to his wife.

The young man borrowed a pencil from the waiter and commenced to multiply $2.50 by one thousand. That was easy. Ten percent of that was two hundred and fifty dollars. Five times that was twelve hundred and fifty dollars. Deduct seven hundred and fifty dollars for the advance. That left five hundred dollars earned by the first printing.

Now there was the second printing. Say that was two thousand. That was twelve and a half percent of five thousand dollars. If that was how the contract was. That would be six hundred and twenty-five dollars. But maybe it did not go up to twelve and a half percent until ten thousand. Well it was still five hundred dollars. That would still leave a thousand.

He started to read the reviews and found that he had drunk the vermouth without ever noticing it. He ordered another and returned the pencil to the waiter. He was still reading the reviews when the girl came in bringing her heavy envelope of letters.

"I didn't know they'd come," she said. "Let me see them. Please let me see them."

The waiter brought her a vermouth and putting it down saw the picture as the girl unfolded a clipping.

"C'est Monsieur?" he asked.

"Yes it is," the girl said and held it up for him to see.

"But differently dressed," the waiter said. "Do they write about the marriage? May I see a picture of Madame?"

"Not about the marriage. Criticisms of a book by Monsieur."

"Magnificent," said the waiter who was deeply moved. "Is Madame also a writer?"

"No," the girl said not looking up from the clippings. "Madame is a housewife."

The waiter laughed proudly. "Madame is probably in the cinema."

They both read clippings and then the girl put the one she was reading down and said, "I'm frightened by them and all the things they say. How can we be us and have the things we have and do what we do and you be this that's in the clippings?"

"I've had them before," the young man said. "They're bad for you but it doesn't last."

"They're terrible," she said. "They could destroy you if you thought about them or believed them. You don't think I married you because you are what they say you are in these clippings do you?"

"No. I want to read them and then we'll seal them up in the envelope."

"I know you have to read them. I don't want to be stupid about them. But even in an envelope it's awful to have them with us. It's like bringing along somebody's ashes in a jar."

"Plenty of people would be happy if their damned husbands had good reviews."

"I'm not plenty of people and you're not my damned husband. I know I'm a violent girl and you're violent too. Please let's not fight. You read them and if there's anything good you tell me and if they say anything about the book that's intelligent that we don't know you tell me."

"The book's made some money already," he told her.

"That's wonderful. I'm so glad. But we know it's good. If the reviews had said it was worthless and it never made a cent I would have been just as proud and just as happy."

I wouldn't, the young man thought. But he did not say it. He went on reading the reviews, unfolding them and folding them up again and putting them back in the envelope. The girl sat opening envelopes and reading her letters without interest. Then she looked out of the cafe at the sea. Her face was a dark gold brown and she had brushed her hair straight back from her forehead the way the sea had pulled it when she had come out of the water and where it was cropped close and on her cheeks the sun had burned it to white gold against the brown of her skin. She looked out at the sea and her eyes were very sad. Then she went back to opening letters. There was one long typewritten one that she read with concentration. Then she went on opening and reading the other letters. The young man looked at her and thought she looked a little as though she were shelling peas.

"What was in the letters?" the young man asked.

"There were checks in some."

"Big ones?"

"Two."

"That's fine," he said.

"Don't go away like that. You always said it never made any difference."

"Have I said anything?"

"No. You just went away."

"I'm sorry," he said. "How big are they?"

"Not much really. But good for us. They've been deposited. It's because I'm married. I told you it was the best thing for us to be married. I know it doesn't mean anything as capital but this is spendable. We can spend it and it doesn't hurt anybody and it's for that. It doesn't have anything to do with regular income nor what I get if I live to be twenty-five or if I ever live to be thirty. This is ours for anything we want to do. Neither of us will have to worry about balances for a while. It's that simple."

"The book has paid back the advance and made about a thousand dollars," he said.

"Isn't that awfully good when it's only just come out?"

"It's all right. Should we have another one of these?" he asked.

"Let's drink something else."

"How much vermouth did you drink?"

"Only the one. I must say it was dull."

"I drank two and didn't even taste them."

"What is there that's real?" she said.

"Did you ever drink Armagnac and soda? That's real enough."

"Good. Let's try that."

The waiter brought the Armagnac and the young man told him to bring a cold bottle of Perrier water instead of the syphon. The waiter poured two large Armagnacs and the young man put ice in the big glasses and poured in the Perrier.

"This will fix us," he said. "It's a hell of a thing to drink before lunch though."

The girl took a long sip. "It's good," she said. "It has a fresh clean healthy ugly taste." She took another long sip. "I can really feel it. Can you?"

"Yes," he said and took a deep breath. "I can feel it."

She drank from the glass again and smiled and the laugh wrinkles came at the corner of her eyes. The cold Perrier had made the heavy brandy alive.

"For heroes," he said.

"I don't mind being a hero," she said. "We're not like other people. We don't have to call each other darling or my dear or my love nor any of that to make a point. Darling and my dearest and my very dearest and all that are obscene to me and we call each other by our Christian names. You know what I'm trying to say. Why do we have to do other things like everyone does?"

"You're a very intelligent girl."

"All right Davie," she said. "Why do we have to be stuffy? Why don't we keep on and travel now when it can never be more fun? We'll do everything you want. If you'd been a European with a lawyer my money would have been yours anyway. It *is* yours."

"The hell with it."

"All right. The hell with it. But we'll spend it and I think it's wonderful. You can write afterwards. That way we can have the fun before I have a baby for one thing. How do I know when I'll have a baby even? Now it's all getting dull and dusty talking about it. Can't we just do it and not talk about it?"

"What if I want to write? The minute you're not going to do something it will probably make you want to do it."

"Then write, stupid. You didn't say you wouldn't write. Nobody said anything about worrying if you wrote. Did they?"

But somewhere something had been said and now he could not remember it because he had been thinking ahead.

"If you want to write go ahead and I'll amuse myself. I don't have to leave you when you write do I?"

"But where would you like us to go now when people begin to come here?"

"Anywhere you want to go. Will you do it, David?"

"For how long?"

"For as long as we want. Six months. Nine months. A year."

"All right," he said.

"Really?"

"Sure."

"You're awfully good. If I didn't love you for anything else I'd love you for decisions."

"They're easy to make when you haven't seen how too many of them can turn out."

He drank the hero drink but it did not taste so good and he ordered a fresh bottle of cold Perrier and made a short drink without ice.

"Make me one please. Short like yours. And then let's let it start and have lunch."

Chapter Three

THAT NIGHT IN BED when they were still awake she said in the dark, "We don't always have to do the devil things either. Please know that."

"I know."

"I love it the way we were before and I'm always your girl. Don't ever be lonely. You know that. I'm how you want but I'm how I want too and it isn't as though it wasn't for us both. You don't have to talk. I'm only telling a story to put you to sleep because you're my good lovely husband and my brother too. I love you and when we go to Africa I'll be your African girl too."

"Are we going to Africa?"

"Aren't we? Don't you remember? That was what it was about today. So we could go there or anywhere. Isn't that where we're going?"

"Why didn't you say it?"

"I didn't want to interfere. I said wherever you wanted. I'd go anywhere. But I thought that was where you wanted."

"It's too early to go to Africa now. It's the big rains and afterwards the grass is too high and it's very cold."

"We could go to bed and keep warm and hear the rain on a tin roof."

"No, it's too early. The roads turn to mud and you can't get around and everything is like a swamp and the grass gets so tall you can't see."

"Then where should we go?"

"We can go to Spain but Sevilla is over and so is San Isidro in Madrid and it's early for there too. It's too early for the Basque coast. It's still cold and rainy. It rains everywhere there now."

"Isn't there a hot part where we could swim the way we do here?"

"You can't swim in Spain the way we do here. You'd get arrested."

"What a bore. Let's wait to go there then because I want us to get darker."

"Why do you want to be so dark?"

"I don't know. Why do you want anything? Right now it's the thing that I want most. That we don't have I mean. Doesn't it make you excited to have me getting so dark?"

"Uh-huh. I love it."

"Did you think I could ever be this dark?"

"No, because you're blond."

"I can because I'm lion color and they can go dark. But I want every part of me dark and it's getting that way and you'll be darker than an Indian and that takes us further away from other people. You see why it's important."

"What will we be?"

"I don't know. Maybe we'll just be us. Only changed. That's maybe the best thing. And we will keep on won't we?"

"Sure. We can go over by the Estérel and explore and find another place the way we found this one."

"We can do that. There are lots of wild places and nobody is there in the summer. We could get a car and then we could go everywhere. Spain too when we want. Once we're really dark it won't be hard to keep unless we had to live in towns. We don't want to be in towns in the summer."

"How dark are you going to get?"

"As dark as I can. We'll have to see. I wish I had some Indian blood. I'm going to be so dark you won't be able to stand it. I can't wait to go up on the beach tomorrow."

She went to sleep that way with her head back and her chin up as though she were in the sun on the beach, breathing softly, and then she curled toward him on her side and the young man lay awake and thought about the day. It is very possible that I couldn't get started, he thought, and it probably is sound to not think about it at all and just enjoy what we have. When I have to work I will. Nothing can stop that. The last book is good and I must make a better one now. This nonsense that we do is fun although I don't know how much of it is nonsense and how much is serious. Drinking brandy at noon is no damn good and already the simple aperitifs mean nothing. That is not a good sign. She changes from a girl into a boy and back to a girl care-lessly and happily. She sleeps easily and beautifully and you will sleep too because all you truly know is that you feel good. You did not sell anything for the money, he thought. Everything she said about the money was true. Actually it all was true. Every-thing was free for a time.

What was it that she had said about destruction? He could not remember that. She'd said it but he could not remember it.

Then he was tired of trying to remember and he looked at the girl and kissed her cheek very lightly and she did not wake. He loved her very much and everything about her and he went to sleep thinking about her cheek against his lips and how the next day they would both be darker from the sun and how dark can she become, he thought, and how dark will she ever really be?

BOOK TWO

Chapter Four

IT WAS LATE AFTERNOON and the small low car came down from the black road across the hills and headlands with the dark blue ocean always on the right onto a deserted boulevard that bordered a flat beach of two miles of yellow sand at Hendaye. Well ahead on the ocean side was the bulk of a big hotel and a casino and on the left there were newly planted trees and Basque villas whitewashed and brown timbered set in their own trees and plantings. The two young people in the car rode down the boulevard slowly looking out at the magnificent beach and at the mountains of Spain that showed blue in this light as the car passed the casino and the big hotel and went on toward the end of the boulevard. Ahead was the mouth of the river that flowed into the ocean. The tide was out and across the bright sand they saw the ancient Spanish town and the green hills across the bay and, at the far point, the lighthouse. They stopped the car.

"It's a lovely place," the girl said.

"There's a cafe with tables under the trees," the young man said. "Old trees."

"The trees are strange," the girl said. "It's all new planting. I wonder why they planted mimosas."

"To compete with where we've come from."

"I suppose so. It all looks awfully new. But it's a wonderful beach. I never saw such a big beach in France nor with such smooth and fine sand. Biarritz is a horror. Let's drive up by the cafe."

They drove back up the right side of the road. The young man pulled the car to the curb and killed the ignition. They crossed to the outdoor cafe and it was pleasant to eat by themselves and be conscious of the people that they did not know eating at the other tables.

That night the wind rose and in their corner room high up in the big hotel they heard the heavy fall of the surf on the beach. In the dark the young man pulled a light blanket up over the sheet and the girl said, "Aren't you glad we decided to stay?"

"I like to hear the surf pound."

"So do I."

They lay close together and listened to the sea. Her head was on his chest and she moved it against his chin and then moved up in the bed and put her cheek against his and pressed it there. She kissed him and he could feel her hand touching him.

"That's good," she said in the darkness. "That's lovely. You're sure you don't want me to change?"

"Not now. Now I'm cold. Please hold me warm."

"I love you when you feel cold against me."

"If it gets this cold here at night we'll have to wear pyjama tops. That will be fun for breakfast in bed."

"It's the Atlantic ocean," she said. "Listen to it."

"We'll have a good time while we're here," he told her. "If you want we'll stay a while. If you want we'll go. There are plenty of places to go."

"We might stay a few days and see."

"Good. If we do I'd like to start to write."

"That would be wonderful. We'll look around tomorrow. You could work here in the room if I were out couldn't you? Until we found some place?"

"Sure."

"You know you must never worry about me because I love you and we're us against all the others. Please kiss me," she said.

He kissed her.

"You know I haven't done anything bad to us. I had to do it. You know that."

He did not say anything and listened to the weight of the surf falling on the hard wet sand in the night.

The next morning there was still heavy surf and the rain came in gusts. They could not see the Spanish coast and when it cleared between the driven squalls of rain and they could see across the angry sea in the bay there were heavy clouds that came down to the base of the mountains. Catherine had gone out in a raincoat after breakfast and had left him to work in the room. It had gone so simply and easily that he thought it was probably worthless. Be careful, he said to himself, it is all very well for you to write simply and the simpler the better. But do not start to think so damned simply. Know how complicated it is and then state it simply. Do you suppose the Grau du Roi time was all simple because you could write a little of it simply?

He went on writing in pencil in the cheap, lined, school notebook that was called a *cahier* and already numbered one in roman numeral. He stopped finally and put the notebook in a suitcase with a cardboard box of pencils and the cone-shaped sharpener, leaving the five pencils he had dulled to point up for the next day, and took his raincoat from the hanger in the closet and walked down the stairs to the lobby of the hotel. He looked into the hotel bar which was gloomy and pleasant in the rain and already had some customers and left his key at the desk. The assistant concierge reached into the mailbox as he hung up the key and said, "Madame left this for Monsieur."

He opened the note which said, David, didn't want to disturb you am at the cafe love Catherine. He put on the old trench coat, found a *boina* in the pocket and walked out of the hotel into the rain.

She was at a corner table in the small cafe and before her was a clouded yellow-tinged drink and a plate with one small dark red freshwater crayfish and the debris of others. She was very far ahead of him. "Where have you been, stranger?"

"Just down the road a piece." He noticed that her face was rain-washed and he concentrated on what rain did to heavily tanned skin. She looked very nice too in spite of it and he was happy to see her this way.

"Did you get going?" the girl asked.

"Good enough."

"You worked then. That's fine."

The waiter had been serving three Spaniards who were sitting at a table next to the door. He came over now holding a glass and an ordinary Pernod bottle and a small narrow-lipped pitcher of water. There were lumps of ice in the water. *"Pour Monsieur aussi?"* he asked.

"Yes," the young man said. "Please."

The waiter poured their high glasses half full of the off-yellow liquid and started to pour the water slowly into the girl's glass. But the young man said, "I'll do it," and the waiter took the bottle away. He seemed relieved to be taking it away and the young man poured the water in a very thin stream and the girl watched the absinthe cloud opalescently. It felt warm as her fingers held the glass and then as it lost the yellow cast and began to look milky it cooled sharply and the young man let the water fall in a drop at a time.

"Why does it have to go in so slowly?" the girl asked.

"It breaks up and goes to pieces if the water pours in too fast," he explained. "Then it's flat and worthless. There ought to be a glass on top with ice and just a little hole for the water to drip. But everybody would know what it was then."

"I had to drink up fast before because two G.N.'s were in," the girl said.

"G.N.'s?"

"Whatyoumacallits nationals. In khaki with bicycles and black leather pistol holsters. I had to engulf the evidence."

"Engulp?"

"Sorry. Once I engulped it I can't say it."

"You want to be careful about absinthe."

"It only makes me feel easier about things."

"And nothing else does?"

He finished making the absinthe for her, holding it well short of mildness. "Go ahead," he told her. "Don't wait for me." She took a long sip and then he took her glass from her and drank and said, "Thank you, Ma'am. That puts heart in a man."

"So make your own, you clipping reader," she said.

"What was that?" the young man said to her.

"I didn't say it."

But she had said it and he said to her, "Why don't you just shut up about the clippings."

"Why?" she said, leaning toward him and speaking too loudly. "Why should I shut up? Just because you wrote this morning? Do you think I married you because you're a writer? You and your clippings."

"All right," the young man said. "Can you tell me the rest of it when we're by ourselves?"

"Don't ever think for a moment I won't," she said.

"I guess not," he said.

"Don't guess," she said. "You can be certain."

David Bourne stood up and went over to the hanger and lifted his raincoat and went out the door without looking back.

At the table Catherine raised her glass and tasted the absinthe very carefully and went on tasting it in little sips.

The door opened and David came back in and walked up to the table. He was wearing his trench coat and had his *boina* pulled low on his forehead. "Do you have the keys to the car?"

"Yes," she said.

"May I have them?"

She gave them to him but said, "Don't be stupid, David. It was the rain and you being the only one who had worked. Sit down."

"Do you want me to?"

"Please," she said.

He sat down. That didn't make much sense, he thought. You got up to go out and take the damned car and stay out and the hell with her and then you come back in and have to ask for the key and then sit down like a slob. He picked up his glass and took a drink. The drink was good anyway.

"What are you going to do about lunch?" he asked.

"You say where and I'll eat it with you. You do still love me, don't you?"

"Don't be silly."

"That was a sordid quarrel," Catherine said.

"The first one too."

"It was my fault about the clippings."

"Let's not mention the god damned clippings."

"That's what it was all about."

"It was you thinking about them when you were drinking. Bringing them up because you were drinking."

"It sounds like regurgitating," she said. "Awful. Actually my tongue just slipped making a joke."

"You had to have them in your head to bring them out that way."

"All right," she said. "I thought maybe it was all over."

"It is."

"Well why do you keep on insisting and insisting about it for then?"

"We shouldn't have taken this drink."

"No. Of course not. Especially me. But you certainly needed it. Do you think it will do you any good?"

"Do we have to do this now?" he asked.

"I'm certainly going to stop it. It bores me."

"That's the one damned word in the language I can't stand."

"Lucky you with only one word like that in the language."

"Oh shit," he said. "Eat lunch by yourself."

"No. I won't. We'll eat lunch together and behave like human beings."

"All right."

"I'm sorry. It really was a joke and it just misfired. Truly David that was all."

Chapter Five

THE TIDE WAS FAR OUT when David Bourne woke and the sun was bright on the beach and the sea was a dark blue. The hills showed green and new washed and the clouds had gone from the mountains. Catherine was still sleeping and he looked at her and watched her regular breathing and the sun on her face and thought, how strange that the sun on her eyes should not wake her.

After he had taken a shower and brushed his teeth and shaved, he was hungry for breakfast but he pulled on a pair of shorts and a sweater and found his notebook and pencils and the sharpener and sat at the table by the window that looked out over the estuary of the river to Spain. He started to write and he forgot about Catherine and what he saw from the window and the writing went by itself as it did with him when he was lucky. He wrote it exactly and the sinister part only showed as the light feathering of a smooth swell on a calm day marking the reef beneath.

When he had worked for a time, he looked at Catherine, still sleeping, her lips smiling now and the rectangle of sunlight from the open window falling across the brown of her body and lighting her dark face and tawny head against the rumpled white of the sheet and the unused pillow. It's too late to get breakfast now, he thought. I'll leave a note and go down to the cafe and get a café crème and something. But while he was putting his work away Catherine woke and came over to him as he was closing the suitcase and put her arms around him and kissed him on the back of his neck and said, "I'm your lazy naked wife."

"What did you wake up for?"

"I don't know. But tell me where you're going and I'll be there in five minutes."

"I'm going to the cafe to get some breakfast."

"Go ahead and I'll join you. You worked didn't you?"

"Sure."

"Weren't you wonderful to after yesterday and everything. I'm so proud. Kiss me and look at us in the mirror on the bathroom door."

He kissed her and they looked into the full length mirror.

"It's so nice not to feel overdressed," she said. "You be good and don't get in any trouble on your way to the cafe. Order me an *oeuf au jambon* too. Don't wait for me. I'm sorry I made you wait so long for breakfast."

At the cafe he found the morning paper and the Paris papers of the day before and had his coffee and milk and the Bayonne ham with a big beautifully fresh egg that he ground coarse pepper over sparsely and spread a little mustard on before he broke the yolk. When Catherine had not come and her egg was in danger of getting cold he ate it too, swabbing the flat dish clean with a piece of the fresh baked bread.

"Here comes Madame," the waiter said. "I'll bring another *plat* for her."

She had put on a skirt and cashmere sweater and pearls and

toweled her head but combed it damp and straight and wet and the tawny color of her hair did not show to make the contrast with her incredibly darkened face. "It's such a beautiful day," she said. "I'm sorry to be late."

"Where are you dressed for?"

"Biarritz. I thought I'd drive in. Do you want to come?"

"You want to go alone."

"Yes," she said. "But you're welcome."

As he stood she said, "I'm going to bring you back a surprise."

"No, don't."

"Yes. And you'll like it."

"Let me go along and keep you from doing anything crazy."

"No. It's better if I do it alone. I'll be back in the afternoon. And don't wait for lunch."

David read the papers and then walked out through the town looking for chalets that might be for rent or for a part of town that might be good to live in and found the newly built up area pleasant but dull. He loved the view across the bay and the estuary to the Spanish side and the old gray stone of Fuenterrabiá and shining white of the houses that spread out from it and the brown mountains with the blue shadows. He wondered why the storm had gone so quickly and thought it must have been only the northern edge of a storm that came in across the Bay of Biscay. Biscay was Vizcaya but that was the Basque province further down the coast well beyond San Sebastian. The mountains that he saw beyond the roofs of the border town of Irun were in Guipúzcoa and beyond them would be Navarra and Navarra was Navarre. And what are we doing here, he thought, and what am I doing walking through a beach resort town looking at newly planted magnolias and bloody mimosas and watching for to-rent signs on phony Basque villas? You didn't work hard enough this morning to make your brain that stupid or are you just hung over from yesterday? You didn't work at all really.

And you better soon because everything's going too fast and you're going with it and you'll be through before ever you know it. Maybe you're through now. All right. Don't start. At least you remember that much. And he walked on through the town, his vision sharpened by spleen and tempered by the ash beauty of the day.

The breeze from the sea was blowing through the room and he was reading with his shoulders and the small of his back against two pillows and another folded behind his head. He was sleepy after lunch but he felt hollow with waiting for her and he read and waited. Then he heard the door open and she came in and for an instant he did not know her. She stood there with her hands below her breasts on the cashmere sweater and breathing as though she had been running.

"Oh, no," she said. "No."

Then she was on the bed pushing her head against him saying, "No. No. Please David. Don't you at all?"

He held her head close against his chest and felt it smooth close clipped and coarsely silky and she pushed it hard against him again and again.

"What did you do, Devil?"

She raised her head and looked at him and her lips pressed against his and she moved them from side to side and moved on the bed so her body was pressed against his.

"Now I can tell," she said. "I'm so glad. It was such a big chance. I'm your new girl now so we'd better find out."

"Let me see."

"I'll show you but let me go a minute."

She came back and stood by the bed with the sun on her through the window. She had dropped the skirt and was barefoot wearing only the sweater and the pearls.

"Take a good look," she said. "Because this is how I am."

He took a good look at the long dark legs the straight standing body the dark face and the sculptured tawny head and she looked at him and said, "Thank you."

"How did you do it?"

"Can I tell you in bed?"

"If you tell me in a hurry."

"No. Not in a hurry. Let me tell. First I had the idea on the road somewhere after Aix en Provence. At Nîmes when we were walking in the garden I think. But I didn't know how it would work or how to tell them how to do it. Then I thought it out and yesterday I decided."

David stroked his hand over her head from her neck over the top of her head to her forehead.

"Let me tell," she said. "I knew they must have good coiffeurs in Biarritz because of the English. So when I got there I went to the best place and I told the coiffeur that I wanted it all brushed forward and he brushed it and it came down to my nose and I could hardly see through it and I said I wanted it cut like a boy when he would first go to public school. He asked me what school so I said Eton or Winchester because they were the only schools I could remember except Rugby and I didn't want Rugby certainly. He said which. So I said Eton but forward all the way. So after he was finished and I looked like the most attractive girl who ever went to Eton I just had him keep on shortening it until Eton was all gone and then I had him keep on shortening it. Then he said very severely that is *not* an Eton crop, Mademoiselle. And I said I didn't want an Eton crop, Monsieur. That was the only way I knew how to explain what I wanted and it is Madame not Mademoiselle. So then I had him shorten it some more and then I kept him shortening it and it is either wonderful or terrible. You don't mind it on my forehead? When it was Eton it fell in my eye."

"It's wonderful."

"It's awfully classic," she said. "But it feels like an animal. Feel it."

He felt it.

"Don't worry about it being too classic," she said. "My mouth balances it. Now can we make love?"

She bent her head forward and he pulled the sweater over her head and down off her arms and bent over her neck to unhook the safety clasp.

"No leave them."

She lay back on the bed her brown legs tight together and her head against the flat sheet the pearls slanted away from the dark rise of her breasts. Her eyes were shut and her arms were by her sides. She *was* a new girl and he saw her mouth was changed too. She was breathing very carefully and she said, "You do everything. From the beginning. From the very beginning."

"Is this the beginning?"

"Oh yes. And don't wait too long. No don't wait—"

In the night she lay curled around him with her head below his chest and stroked it softly across him from one flank to another and then came up to put her lips on his and put her arms around him and said, "You're so lovely and loyal when you are asleep and you didn't wake and didn't wake. I thought you wouldn't and it was lovely. You were so loyal to me. Did you think it was a dream? Don't wake. I'm going to sleep but if I don't I'll be a wild girl. She stays awake and takes care of you. You sleep and know I'm here. Please sleep."

In the morning when he woke there was the lovely body that he knew close against him and he looked and saw the waxed-wood dark shoulders and neck and the fair tawny head close and smooth lying as a small animal and he shifted down in the bed and turned toward her and kissed her forehead with her hair under his lips and then her eyes and then gently, her mouth.

"I'm asleep."

"So was I."

"I know. Feel how strange. All night it was wonderful how strange."

"Not strange."

"Say so if you want. Oh we fit so wonderfully. Can we both go to sleep?"

"Do you want to be asleep?"

"Us both asleep."

"I'll try."

"Are you asleep?"

"No."

"Please try."

"I'm trying."

"Shut your eyes then. How can you sleep if you won't shut your eyes?"

"I like to see you in the morning all new and strange."

"Was I good to invent it?"

"Don't talk."

"It's the only way to slow things. I have already. Couldn't you tell? Of course you could. Couldn't you tell now and now and now like our hearts beating together it is the same I know it's only that that counts but we don't count it's so lovely and so good so good and lovely—"

She came back to the big room and went to the mirror and sat and brushed her hair looking at herself critically.

"Let's have breakfast in bed," she said. "And can we have champagne if it's not wicked? In the brut they have Lanson and Perrier-Jouët of the good. May I ring?"

"Yes," he said and went under the shower. Before he put it on full force he could hear her voice on the telephone.

When he came out she was sitting back very formally against two pillows with all the pillows neatly shaken out and placed two and two at the head of the bed.

"Do I look all right with my head wet?"

"It's just damp. You dried it with the towel."

"I can cut it shorter on the forehead. I can do that myself. Or you can."

"I'd like it if it came over your eyes."

"Maybe it will," she said. "Who knows? Maybe we'll get tired of being classical. And today we'll stay on the beach all through noon. We'll go way far down it and we can tan really when the people all come in for lunch and then we'll ride to St. Jean to eat when we're hungry at the Bar Basque. But first you'll make us go to the beach because we need to."

"Good."

David moved a chair over and put his hand close on hers and she looked at him and said, "Two days ago I understood everything and then the absinthe made me turn on it."

"I know," David told her. "You couldn't help it."

"But I hurt you about the clippings."

"No," he said. "You tried. You didn't make it."

"I'm so sorry, David. Please believe me."

"Everybody has strange things that mean things to them. You couldn't help it."

"No," the girl said and shook her head.

"It's all right then," David said. "Don't cry. It's all right."

"I never cry," she said. "But I can't help it."

"I know it and you're beautiful when you cry."

"No. Don't say it. But I never cried before did I?"

"Never."

"But will it be bad for you if we stay here just two days on the beach? We haven't had any chance to swim and it would be silly to have been here and not to swim. Where are we going to go when we leave here? Oh. We haven't decided yet. We'll probably decide tonight or in the morning. Where would you suggest?"

"I think anywhere would be fine," David said.

"Well maybe that's where we will go."

"It's a big place."

"It's nice to be alone though and I'll pack us nicely."

"There's nothing much to do except put in toilet things and close two bags."

"We can leave in the morning if you want. Truly I don't want to do anything to you or have any bad effect on you."

The waiter knocked on the door.

"There was no more Perrier-Jouët, Madame, so I brought the Lanson."

She had stopped crying and David's hand was still close on hers and he said, "I know."

Chapter Six

THEY HAD SPENT the morning at the Prado and now were sitting at a place in a building with thick stone walls. It was cool and very old. There were wine casks around the walls. The tables were old and thick and the chairs were worn. The light came from the door. The waiter brought them glasses of manzanilla from the lowland near Cádiz called the Marismas with thin slices of *jamón serrano,* a smoky, hard cured ham from pigs that fed on acorns, and bright red spicy *salchichón,* another even spicier dark sausage from a town called Vich and anchovies and garlic olives. They ate these and drank more of the manzanilla, which was light and nutty tasting.

Catherine had a Spanish-English Method book with a green cover on the table close to her hand and David had a stack of the morning papers. It was a hot day but cool in the old building and the waiter asked, "Do you want gazpacho?" He was an old man and he filled their glasses again.

"Do you think the señorita would like it?"

"Try her," the waiter said gravely as though he were speaking of a mare.

It came in a large bowl with ice floating with the slices of crisp cucumber, tomato, garlic bread, green and red peppers, and the coarsely peppered liquid that tasted lightly of oil and vinegar.

"It's a salad soup," Catherine said. "It's delicious."

"*Es gazpacho,*" the waiter said.

They drank Valdepeñas now from a big pitcher and it started to build with the foundation of the *marismeño* only held back temporarily by the dilution of the gazpacho which it moved in on confidently. It built solidly.

"What is this wine?" Catherine asked.

"It's an African wine," David said.

"They always say that Africa begins at the Pyrenees," Catherine said. "I remember how impressed I was when I first heard it."

"That's one of those easy sayings," David said. "It's more complicated than that. Just drink it."

"But how can I tell about where Africa begins if I've never been there? People are always telling you tricky things."

"Sure. You can tell."

"The Basque country certainly wasn't like Africa or anything I ever heard about Africa."

"Neither is Asturias nor Galicia but once you're in from the coast it gets to be Africa fast enough."

"But why didn't they ever paint that country?" Catherine asked. "In all the backgrounds it is always the mountains out by the Escorial."

"The sierra," David said. "Nobody wanted to buy pictures of Castilla the way you saw it. They never did have landscape painters. The painters painted what was ordered."

"Except Greco's Toledo. It's terrible to have such a wonderful country and no good painters ever paint it," Catherine said.

"What should we eat after the gazpacho?" David said. The

proprietor, who was a short middle-aged man, heavily built and square faced, had come over. "He thinks we ought to have meat of some kind."

"*Hay solomillo muy bueno,*" the owner insisted.

"No, please," Catherine said. "Just a salad."

"Well, at least drink a little wine," the proprietor said and refilled the pitcher from the spigot of the cask behind the bar.

"I shouldn't drink," Catherine said. "I'm sorry I'm talking so much. I'm sorry if I talked stupidly. I usually do."

"You talk very interestingly and awfully well for a hot day like this. Does the wine make you talkative?"

"It's a different sort of talkative than absinthe," Catherine said. "It doesn't feel dangerous. I've started on my good new life and I'm reading now and looking outward and trying not to think about myself so much and I'm going to keep it up but we ought not to be in any town this time of year. Maybe we'll go. The whole way here I saw wonderful things to paint and I can't paint at all and never could. But I know wonderful things to write and I can't even write a letter that isn't stupid. I never wanted to be a painter nor a writer until I came to this country. Now it's just like being hungry all the time and there's nothing you can ever do about it."

"The country is here. You don't have to do anything about it. It's always here. The Prado's here," David said.

"There's nothing except through yourself," she said. "And I don't want to die and it be gone."

"You have every mile we drove. All the yellow country and the white hills and the chaff blowing and the long lines of poplars by the road. You know what you saw and what you felt and it's yours. Don't you have le Grau du Roi and Aigues Mortes and all the Camargue that we rode through on our bikes? This will be the same."

"But what about when I'm dead?"

"Then you're dead."

"But I can't stand to be dead."

"Then don't let it happen till it happens. Look at things and listen and feel."

"What if I can't remember?"

He had spoken about death as though it did not matter. She drank the wine and looked at the thick stone walls in which there were only small windows with bars high up that gave onto a narrow street where the sun did not shine. The doorway, though, gave onto an arcade and the bright sunlight on the worn stones of the square.

"When you start to live outside yourself," Catherine said, "it's all dangerous. Maybe I'd better go back into our world, your and my world that I made up; we made up I mean. I was a great success in that world. It was only four weeks ago. I think maybe I will be again."

The salad came and then there was its greenness on the dark table and the sun on the plaza beyond the arcade.

"Do you feel better?" David asked.

"Yes," she said. "I was thinking so much about myself that I was getting impossible again, like a painter and I was my own picture. It was awful. Now that I'm all right again I hope it still lasts."

It had rained hard and now the heat was broken. They were in the cool shutter-slatted dimness of the big room in The Palace and had bathed together in the deep water in the long deep tub and then had turned the plug and let the full force of the water splash and flow over them, swirling as it drained away. They had blotted each other with the huge towels and then come to the bed. As they lay on the bed there was a cool breeze that came through the slats of the blinds and moved over them. Catherine lay propped on her elbows with her chin on her hands. "Do you think it would be fun if I went back to being a boy again? It wouldn't be any trouble."

"I like you the way you are now."

"It's sort of tempting. But I shouldn't do it in Spain I suppose. It's such a formal country."

"Stay the way you are."

"What makes your voice be different when you say it? I think I'll do it."

"No. Not now."

"Thank you for the not now. Should I make love this time as a girl and then do it?"

"You're a girl. You are a girl. You're my lovely girl Catherine."

"Yes I am your girl and I love you and I love you and I love you."

"Don't talk."

"Yes I will. I'm your girl Catherine and I love you please I love you always always always—"

"You don't have to keep saying it. I can tell."

"I like to say it and I have to say it and I've been a fine girl and a good girl and I will again. I promise I will again."

"You don't have to say it."

"Oh yes I do. I say it and I said it and you said it. You now please. Please you."

They lay quiet for a long time and she said, "I love you so much and you're such a good husband."

"You blessed."

"Was I what you wanted?"

"What do you think?"

"I hope I was."

"You were."

"I promised truly and I will and I'll keep it. Now can I be a boy again?"

"Why?"

"Just for a little while."

"Why?"

"I loved it and I don't miss it but I'd like to be again in bed at night if it isn't bad for you. Can I be again? If it's not bad for you?"

"The hell with if it's bad for me."

"Then can I?"

"Do you really want to?"

He had kept from saying have to so she said, "I don't have to but please if it's all right. Can I please?"

"All right." He kissed her and held her to him.

"Nobody can tell which way I am but us. I'll only be a boy at night and won't embarrass you. Don't worry about it please."

"All right, boy."

"I lied when I said I didn't have to. It came so suddenly today."

He shut his eyes and did not think and she kissed him and it had gone further now and he could tell and feel the desperateness.

"Now you change. Please. Don't make me change you. Must I? All right I will. You're changed now. You are. You did it too. You are. You did it too. I did it to you but you did it. Yes you did. You're my sweet dearest darling Catherine. You're my sweet my lovely Catherine. You're my girl my dearest only girl. Oh thank you thank you my girl—"

She lay there a long time and he thought that she had gone to sleep. Then she moved away very slowly lifting herself lightly on her elbows and said, "I have a wonderful surprise for myself for tomorrow. I'm going to the Prado in the morning and see all the pictures as a boy."

"I give up," David said.

Chapter Seven

IN THE MORNING he got up while she was still sleeping and went out into the bright early morning freshness of the high plateau air. He walked in the street up the hill to the Plaza Santa Ana and had breakfast at a cafe and read the local papers. Catherine had wanted to be at the Prado at ten when it opened and before he left he had set the alarm to wake her at nine. Outside on the street, walking up the hill he had thought of her sleeping, the beautiful rumpled head that looked like an ancient coin lying against the white sheet, the pillow pushed away, the upper sheet showing the curves of her body. It lasted a month, he thought, or almost. And the other time from le Grau du Roi to Hendaye was two months. No, less, because she started thinking of it in Nîmes. It wasn't two months. We've been married three months and two weeks and I hope I make her happy always but in this I do not think anybody can take care of anybody. It's enough to stay in it. The difference is that she asked this time, he told himself. She did ask.

When he had read the papers and then paid for his breakfast and walked out into the heat that had come back to the plateau when the wind had changed, he made his way to the cool, formal, sad politeness of the bank, where he found mail that had been forwarded from Paris. He opened and read mail while he waited through the lengthy, many-windowed formalities of cashing a draft which had been sent from his bank to this, their Madrid correspondent.

Finally with the heavy notes buttoned into his jacket pocket he came out into the glare again and stopped at the newsstand to buy the English and American papers that had come in on the morning Sud Express. He bought some bullfight weeklies to wrap the English language papers in and then walked down the Carrera San Geronimo to the cool friendly morning gloom of the Buffet Italianos. There was no one in the place yet and he remembered that he had made no rendezvous with Catherine.

"What will you drink?" the waiter asked him.

"Beer," he said.

"This isn't a beer place."

"Don't you have beer?"

"Yes. But it's not a beer place."

"Up yours," he said and re-rolled the papers and went out and walked across the street and back on the other side to turn to the left into the Calle Vittoria and on to the Cervezería Alvarez. He sat at a table under the awning in the passageway and drank a big cold glass of the draft beer.

The waiter was probably only making conversation, he thought, and what the man said was quite true. It isn't a beer place. He was just being literal. He wasn't being insolent. That was a very bad thing to say and he had no defense against it. It was a shitty thing to do. He drank a second beer and called the waiter to pay.

"Y la Señora?" the waiter said.

"At the Museo del Prado. I'm going to get her."

"Well, until you get back," the waiter said.

He walked back to the hotel by a downhill shortcut. The key was at the desk so he rode up to their floor and left the papers and the mail on a table in the room and locked most of the money in his suitcase. The room was made up and the shutters were lowered against the heat so that the room was darkened. He washed and then sorted through his mail and took four letters out and put them in his hip pocket. He took the Paris editions of *The New York Herald,* the *Chicago Tribune* and the *London Daily Mail* down with him to the bar of the hotel stopping at the desk to leave the key and to ask the clerk to tell Madame, when she came in, that he was in the bar.

He sat on a stool at the bar and ordered a *marismeño* and opened and read his letters while he ate the garlic-flavored olives from the saucer the bartender had placed before him with his glass. One of the letters had two cuttings of reviews of his novel from monthly magazines and he read them with no feeling that they dealt with him or with anything that he had written.

He put the cuttings back in the envelope. They had been understanding and perceptive reviews but to him they had meant nothing. He read the letter from the publisher with the same detachment. The book had sold well and they thought that it might continue selling on into the fall although nobody could ever tell about such things. Certainly, so far, it had received an extraordinarily fine critical reception and the way would be open for his next book. It was a great advantage that this was his second and not his first novel. It was tragic how often first novels were the only good novels American writers had in them. But this, his publisher went on, his second, validated all the promise his first had shown. It was an unusual summer in New York, cold and wet. Oh Christ, David thought, the hell with how it was in New York and the hell with that thin-lipped bastard Coolidge fishing for trout in a high stiff collar in a fish hatchery in the Black Hills we stole from the Sioux and the Cheyenne and bathtub-ginned-up writers wondering if their baby does the Charleston. And the hell with the promise he had validated. What promise to whom? To *The Dial*, to *The Bookman*, to *The New Republic*? No, he had shown it. Let me show you my promise that I'm going to validate it. What shit.

"Hello, young man," said a voice. "What are you looking so indignant about?"

"Hello, Colonel," David said and felt suddenly happy. "What the hell are you doing here?"

The Colonel, who had deep blue eyes, sandy hair and a tanned face that looked as though it had been carved out of flint by a tired sculptor who had broken his chisel on it, picked up David's glass and tasted the *marismeño*.

"Bring me a bottle of whatever this young man is drinking to that table," he said to the bartender. "Bring a cold bottle. You don't need to ice it. Bring it immediately."

"Yes sir," said the bartender. "Very good sir."

"Come along," the Colonel said to David, leading him to the table in the corner of the room. "You're looking very well."

"So are you."

Colonel John Boyle was wearing a dark blue suit of a cloth that looked stiff but cool and a blue shirt and black tie. "I'm always well," he said. "Do you want a job?"

"No," said David.

"Just like that. Don't even ask what it is." His voice sounded as though he had hawked it up out of a dusty throat.

The wine came and the waiter filled two glasses and put down saucers of the garlic olives and of hazelnuts.

"No anchovies?" the Colonel asked. "What sort of a *fonda* is this?"

The bartender smiled and went for the anchovies.

"Excellent wine," the Colonel said. "First rate. I always hoped your taste would improve. Now why don't you want a job? You've just finished a book."

"I'm on my honeymoon."

"Silly expression," the Colonel said. "I never liked it. It sounds sticky. Why didn't you say you've just been married? It makes no difference. You'd be worthless in any event."

"What was the job?"

"No use talking about it now. Who did you marry? Anyone I know?"

"Catherine Hill."

"Knew her father. Very odd type. Killed himself in a car. His wife too."

"I never knew them."

"You never knew him?"

"No."

"Strange. But perfectly understandable. He's no loss to you as a father-in-law. The mother was very lonely they say. Stupid way for grown up people to be killed. Where did you meet this girl?"

"In Paris."

"She has a silly uncle who lives there. He's really worthless. Do you know him?"

"I've seen him at the races."

"At Longchamps and Auteuil. How could you help it?"

"I didn't marry her family."

"Of course not. But you always do. Dead or alive."

"Not the uncles and aunts."

"Well anyway, have fun. You know, I liked the book. Has it done well?"

"It's done pretty well."

"It moved me very deeply," the Colonel said. "You're a deceptive son of a bitch."

"So are you, John."

"I hope so," the Colonel said.

David saw Catherine at the door and stood up. She came over to them and David said, "This is Colonel Boyle."

"How do you do, my dear?"

Catherine looked at him and smiled and sat down at the table. David watched her and it seemed as though she were holding her breath.

"Are you tired?" David asked.

"I think so."

"Have a glass of this," the Colonel said.

"Would it be all right if I had an absinthe?"

"Of course," David said. "I'll have one too."

"Not for me," the Colonel said to the bartender. "This bottle's lost its freshness. Put it back to chill and bring me a glass from a cold bottle."

"Do you like the real Pernod?" he asked Catherine.

"Yes," she said. "I'm shy with people and it helps."

"It's an excellent drink," he said. "I'd join you but I have work I must do after lunch."

"I'm sorry I forgot to make a rendezvous," David said.

"This is very nice."

"I stopped by for the mail at the bank. There's quite a lot for you. I left it in the room."

"I don't care about it," she said.

"I saw you in the Prado looking at the Grecos," the Colonel said.

"I saw you too," she said. "Do you always look at pictures as though you owned them and were deciding how to have them re-hung properly?"

"Probably," the Colonel said. "Do you always look at them as though you were the young chief of a warrior tribe who had gotten loose from his councillors and was looking at that marble of Leda and the Swan?"

Catherine blushed under her dark tan and looked at David and then at the Colonel.

"I like you," she said. "Tell me some more."

"I like you," he said. "And I envy David. Is he everything you want?"

"Don't you know?"

"'To me the visible world is visible,'" the Colonel said. "Now go on and take another sip of that wormwood-tasting truth serum."

"I don't need it now."

"Aren't you shy now? Drink it anyway. It's good for you. You're the darkest white girl I've ever seen. Your father was very dark though."

"I must have his skin. My mother was very fair."

"I never knew her."

"Did you know my father well?"

"Quite well."

"How was he?"

"He was a very difficult and charming man. Are you really shy?"

"Truly. Ask David."

"You get over it awfully quickly."

"You rode over it. How was my father?"

"He was the shyest man I ever knew and he could be the most charming."

"Did he have to use Pernod too?"

"He used everything."

"Do I remind you of him?"

"Not at all."

"That's good. Does David?"

"Not in the least."

"That's even better. How did you know I was a boy in the Prado?"

"Why shouldn't you be?"

"I only started it again last evening. I was a girl for almost a month. Ask David."

"You don't need to say ask David. What are you right now?"

"A boy if it's all right with you."

"It's fine with me. But you're not."

"I just wanted to say it," she said. "Now that I said it I don't have to be it. But it was wonderful in the Prado. That was why I wanted to tell David about it."

"You'll have plenty of time to tell David."

"Yes," she said. "We have time for things."

"Tell me where you got so dark," the Colonel said. "Do you know how dark you are?"

"That was from le Grau du Roi and then not far from la Napoule. There was a cove there with a trail that went down to it through the pines. You couldn't see it from the road."

"How long did it take to get so dark?"

"About three months."

"And what are you going to do with it?"

"Wear it," she said. "It's very becoming in bed."

"I shouldn't think you'd want to waste it in town."

"The Prado isn't wasting. I don't really wear it. It's me. I really am this dark. The sun just develops it. I wish I was darker."

"You probably will be then," the Colonel said. "Do you have other things like that to look forward to?"

"Just every day," Catherine said. "I look forward to every day."

"And has today been a good one?"

"Yes. You know it has. You were there."

"Will you and David lunch with me?"

"All right," Catherine said. "I'll go up and change. Will you wait for me?"

"Don't you want to finish your drink?" David asked.

"I don't care about it," she said. "Don't worry about me. I won't be shy."

She walked to the door and they both looked after her.

"Was I too rough?" the Colonel asked. "I hope not. She's a very lovely girl."

"I just hope I'm good for her."

"You are. How are you doing yourself?"

"All right I think."

"Are you happy?"

"Very."

"Remember everything is right until it's wrong. You'll know when it's wrong."

"You think so?"

"I'm quite sure. If you don't it doesn't matter. Nothing will matter then."

"How fast will it go?"

"I didn't say anything about speed. What are you talking about?"

"Sorry."

"It's what you have, so have a lovely time."

"We do."

"So I see. There's only one thing."

"What?"

"Take good care of her."

"That's all you've got to tell me?"

"One small thing more: The get's no good."

"There isn't any get yet."

"It's kinder to shoot the get."

"Kinder?"

"Better."

They talked about people for a while, the Colonel speaking outrageously, and then David saw Catherine come through the door wearing a white sharkskin outfit to show how really dark she was.

"You do really look extraordinarily beautiful," the Colonel said to Catherine. "But you must try to get darker."

"Thank you. I will," she said. "We don't have to go out now in the heat do we? Can't we sit here in the cool? We can eat here in the grill."

"You're lunching with me," the Colonel said.

"No please. You're lunching with us."

David stood up uncertainly. There were more people at the bar now. Looking down at the table he saw that he had drunk Catherine's drink as well as his own. He did not remember drinking either of them.

It was the siesta time and they lay on the bed and David was reading by the light that came in the window on the left of the bed where he had pulled up one of the slatted curtains about a third of its length. The light was reflected from the building across the street. The curtain was not pulled high enough to show the sky.

"The Colonel liked me being so dark," Catherine said. "We must get to the sea again. I have to keep it."

"We'll go there whenever you want."

"That will be wonderful. Can I tell you something? I have to."

"What?"

"I didn't change back to be a girl for lunch. Did I behave all right?"

"You didn't?"

"No. Do you mind? But now I'm your boy and I'll do anything for you."

David continued reading.

"Are you angry?"

"No." Sobered, he thought.

"It's simpler now."

"I don't think so."

"Then I'll be careful. This morning everything I did felt so right and happy, so clean and good in the daylight. Couldn't I try now and we see?"

"I'd rather you didn't."

"Can I kiss you and try?"

"Not if you're a boy and I'm a boy."

His chest felt as though there were an iron bar inside it from one side to the other. "I wish you hadn't told the Colonel."

"But he saw me, David. He brought it up and he knew all about it and understood. It wasn't stupid to tell him. It was better. He's our friend. If I told him he wouldn't talk. If I didn't tell him he had a right to."

"You can't trust all people like that."

"I don't care about people. I only care about you. I'd never make scandals with other people."

"My chest feels like it is locked in iron."

"I'm sorry. Mine feels so happy."

"My dearest Catherine."

"That's good. You call me Catherine always when you want. I am your Catherine too. I'm always Catherine when you need her. We'd better go to sleep or should we start and see what happens?"

"Let's first lie very quiet in the dark," David said and lowered the latticed shade and they lay side by side on the bed in the big room in The Palace in Madrid where Catherine had walked in the Museo del Prado in the light of day as a boy and now she would show the dark things in the light and there would, it seemed to him, be no end to the change.

Chapter Eight

IN THE BUEN RETIRO in the morning it was as fresh as though it was a forest. It was green and the trunks of the trees were dark and the distances were all new. The lake was not where it had been and when they saw it through the trees it was quite changed.

"You walk ahead," she said. "I want to look at you."

So he turned away from her and walked to where there was a bench and sat down. He could see a lake at a long distance and knew it was too far to ever walk to. He sat there on the bench and she sat down beside him and said, "It's all right."

But remorse had been there to meet him in the Retiro and now it was so bad he told Catherine that he would meet her at the cafe of The Palace.

"Are you all right? Do you want me to come with you?"

"No. I'm all right. I just have to go."

"I'll see you there," she said.

She looked particularly beautiful that morning and she smiled at their secret and he smiled at her and then took his remorse to the cafe. He did not think he would make it but he did and later when Catherine came he was finishing his second absinthe and the remorse was gone.

"How are you, Devil?" he said.

"I'm your devil," she said. "Could I have one of those too?"

The waiter went away pleased to see her looking so handsome and so happy and she said, "What was it?"

"I just felt rotten but I feel fine now."

"Was it that bad?"

"No," he lied.

She shook her head. "I'm so sorry. I hoped there wouldn't be any bad at all."

"It went away."

"That's good. Isn't it lovely to be here in the summer and no one here? I thought of something."

"Already?"

"We can stay on and not go to the sea. This is ours now. The town and here. We could stay here and then drive back straight through to la Napoule."

"There aren't many more moves to make."

"Don't. We've only just started."

"Yes . . . we can always go back where we started."

"Of course we can and we will."

"Let's not talk about it," he said.

He had felt it start to come back and he took a long sip of his drink.

"It's a very strange thing," he said. "This drink tastes exactly like remorse. It has the true taste of it and yet it takes it away."

"I don't like you to have to take it for that. We aren't like that. We mustn't be."

"Maybe I am."

"You mustn't be." She took a long sip out of her glass and another long sip and looked around and then at him. "I can do it. Look at me and watch it happen. Here in the outdoor cafe of

The Palace in Madrid and you can see the Prado and the street and the sprinklers under the trees so it's real. It's awfully brusque. But I can do it. You can see. Look. The lips are your girl again and I'm all the things you really want. Haven't I done it? Tell me."

"You didn't have to."

"Do you like me as a girl," she said very seriously and then smiled.

"Yes," he said.

"That's good," she said. "I'm glad someone likes it because it's a god damned bore."

"Don't do it then."

"Didn't you hear me say I did it? Didn't you watch me do it? Do you want me to wrench myself around and tear myself in two because you can't make up your mind? Because you won't stay with anything?"

"Would you hold it down?"

"Why should I hold it down? You want a girl don't you? Don't you want everything that goes with it? Scenes, hysteria, false accusations, temperament isn't that it? I'm holding it down. I won't make you uncomfortable in front of the waiter. I won't make the waiter uncomfortable. I'll read my damned mail. Can we send up and get my mail?"

"I'll go up and get it."

"No. I shouldn't be here by myself."

"That's right," he said.

"You see? That was why I said to send for it."

"They wouldn't give a *botones* the key to the room. That was why I said I'd go."

"I'm over it," Catherine said. "I'm not going to act that way. Why should I act that way to you? It was ludicrous and undignified. It was so silly I won't even ask you to forgive me. Besides I have to go up to the room anyway."

"Now?"

"Because I'm a god damned woman. I thought if I'd be a girl and stay a girl I'd have a baby at least. Not even that."

"That could be my fault."

"Don't let's ever talk about faults. You stay here and I'll bring back the mail. We'll read our mail and be nice good intelligent American tourists who are disappointed because they came to Madrid at the wrong time of year."

At lunch Catherine said, "We'll go back to la Napoule. There is no one there and we'll be quiet and good and work and take care of each other. We can drive to Aix too and see all the Cézanne country. We didn't stay there long enough before."

"We'll have a lovely time."

"It isn't too soon for you to start to work again is it?"

"No. It would be good to start now. I'm sure."

"That will be wonderful and I'll study Spanish really for when we come back. And I have so much I have to read."

"We have lots to do."

"We'll do it too."

BOOK THREE

Chapter Nine

THE NEW PLAN lasted a little more than a month. They had three rooms at the end of the long low rose-colored Provençal house where they had stayed before. It was in the pines on the Estérel side of la Napoule. Out of the windows there was the sea and from the garden in front of the long house where they ate under the trees they could see the empty beaches, the high papyrus grass at the delta of the small river and across the bay was the white curve of Cannes with the hills and the far mountains behind. There was no one staying at the long house now in summer and the proprietor and his wife were pleased to have them back.

Their bedroom was the big room at the end. It had windows on three sides and was cool that summer. At night they smelled the pines and the sea. David worked in a room at the further end. He started early each morning and when he was finished he would find Catherine and they would go to a cove in the rocks where there was a sand beach to sun and to swim. Sometimes Catherine was gone with the car and he would wait for her and have a drink out on the terrace after his work. It was impossible to drink pastis after absinthe and he had taken to drinking whiskey and Perrier water. This pleased the proprietor, who was now doing a good defensive summer business with the presence of the two Bournes in the dead summer season. He had not hired a cook and his wife was doing the cooking. One maid servant looked after the rooms and a nephew, who was an apprentice waiter, served at table.

Catherine enjoyed driving the small car and went on buying and collecting trips to Cannes and to Nice. The big winter season shops were closed but she found extravagances to eat and solid values to drink and located the places where she could buy books and magazines.

David had worked very hard for four days. They had spent all the afternoon in the sun on the sand of a new cove they had found and they had been in the water until they were both tired and then come home in the evening with salt dried on their backs and in their hair to have a drink and take showers and change.

In bed the breeze came in from the sea. It was cool and they lay side by side in the dark with the sheet over them and Catherine said, "You said I was to tell you."

"I know."

She leaned over him and held his head in her hands and kissed him. "I want to so much. Can I? May I?"

"Sure."

"I'm so happy. I've made a lot of plans," she said. "And this time I'm not going to start so bad and wild."

"What sort of plans?"

"I can tell but it would be better to show it. We could do it tomorrow. Will you go in with me?"

"Where?"

"To Cannes where I went when we were here before. He's a

very good coiffeur. We're friends and he's better than the one in Biarritz because he understood right away."

"What have you been doing?"

"I went to see him this morning while you were working and I explained and he studied it and understood and thought it would be fine. I told him I hadn't decided but that if I did I'd try to get you to have yours cut the same way."

"How is it cut?"

"You'll see. We'll go together. It's sort of bevelled back from the natural line. He's very enthusiastic. I think it's because he's crazy about the Bugatti. Are you afraid?"

"No."

"I can't wait. He wants to lighten it really but we were afraid you might not like it."

"The sun and the salt water lighten it."

"This would be much fairer. He said he could make it as fair as Scandinavian. Think how that would be with our dark skin. And we could make yours lighter too."

"No. I'd feel funny."

"Who do you know here that makes any difference? You'd get lighter swimming all summer anyway."

He did not say anything and she said, "You won't have to. We'll just do mine and maybe you'll want to. We can see."

"Don't make plans, Devil. Tomorrow I'll get up very early and work and you sleep as late as you can."

"Then write for me too," she said. "No matter if it's where I've been bad put in how much I love you."

"I'm nearly up to now."

"Can you publish it or would it be bad to?"

"I've only tried to write it."

"Can I ever read it?"

"If I ever get it right."

"I'm so proud of it already and we won't have any copies for sale and none for reviewers and then there'll never be clippings and you'll never be self conscious and we'll always have it just for us."

David Bourne woke when it was light and put on shorts and a shirt and went outside. The breeze had died. The sea was calm and the day smelled of the dew and the pines. He walked bare footed across the flagstones of the terrace to the room at the far end of the long house and went in and sat down at the table where he worked. The windows had been open overnight and the room was cool and full of early morning promise.

He was writing about the road from Madrid to Zaragossa and the rising and falling of the road as they came at speed into the country of the red buttes and the little car on the then dusty road picked up the Express train and Catherine passed it gently car by car, the tender, and then the engineer and fireman, and finally the nose of the engine, and then she shifted as the road switched left and the train disappeared into a tunnel.

"I had it," she had said. "But it went to ground. Tell me if I can get it again."

He had looked at the Michelin map and said, "Not for a while."

"I'll let it go then and we'll see the country." As the road climbed there were poplar trees along the river and the road climbed steeply and he felt the car accept it and then Catherine shift again happily as it flattened the steep grade.

Later, when he heard her voice in the garden, he stopped writing. He locked the suitcase with the cahiers of manuscript and went out locking the door after him. The girl would use the pass key to clean the room.

Catherine was sitting at breakfast on the terrace. There was a red-and-white checked cloth on the table. She wore her old Grau du Roi striped shirt fresh-washed and shrunk now and much faded, new gray flannel slacks, and espadrilles.

"Hello," she said. "I couldn't sleep late."

"You look lovely."

"Thank you. I feel lovely."

"Where did you get those slacks?"

"I had them made in Nice. By a good tailor. Are they all right?"

"They're very well cut. They just look new. Are you going to wear them into town?"

"Not town. Cannes in the off season. Everybody will next year. People are wearing our shirts now. They're no good with skirts. You don't mind do you?"

"Not at all. They look right. They just looked so well creased."

After breakfast while David shaved and showered and then pulled on a pair of old flannels and a fisherman's shirt and found his espadrilles Catherine put on a blue linen shirt with an open collar and a heavy white linen skirt.

"We're better this way. Even if the slacks are right for here they're too show-off for this morning. We'll save them."

It was very friendly and offhand at the coiffeur's but very professional. Monsieur Jean, who was about David's age and looked more Italian than French, said, "I will cut it as she asks. Do you agree, Monsieur?"

"I don't belong to the syndicate," David said. "I leave it to you two."

"Perhaps we should experiment on Monsieur," Monsieur Jean said. "In case anything goes wrong."

But Monsieur Jean began cutting Catherine's hair very carefully and skillfully and David watched her dark serious face above the smock that came close around her neck. She looked into the hand mirror and watched the comb and scissors lifting and snipping. The man was working like a sculptor, absorbed and serious. "I thought about it all last night and this morning," the coiffeur said. "If you don't believe that, Monsieur, I understand. But this is as important to me as your métier is to you."

He stepped back to look at the shape he was making. Then he snipped more rapidly and finally turned the chair so the big mirror was reflected in the small one Catherine held.

"Do you want it cut that way above the ears?" she asked the coiffeur.

"As you like. I can make it more dégagé if you wish. But it will be beautiful as is if we are going to make it truly fair."

"I want it fair," Catherine said.

He smiled. "Madame and I have spoken of it. But I said it must be Monsieur's decision."

"Monsieur gave his decision," Catherine said.

"How fair did Monsieur say he wished it to be?"

"As fair as you can make it," she said.

"Don't say that," Monsieur Jean said. "You must tell me."

"As fair as my pearls," Catherine said. "You've seen them plenty of times."

David had come over and was watching Monsieur Jean stir a large glassful of the shampoo with a wooden spoon. "I have the shampoos made up with castile soap," the coiffeur said. "It's warm. Please come over here to the basin. Sit forward," he said to Catherine, "and put this cloth across your forehead."

"But it isn't even really a boy's haircut," Catherine said. "I wanted it the way we planned. Everything's going wrong."

"It couldn't be more a boy's haircut. You must believe me."

He was lathering her head now with the foamy thick shampoo with the acrid odor.

When her head had been shampooed and rinsed again and again it looked to David as though it had no color and the water tunnelled through it showing only a wet paleness. The coiffeur put a towel over it and rubbed it softly. He was very sure about it.

"Don't be desperate, Madame," he said. "Why would I do anything against your beauty?"

"I *am* desperate and there isn't any beauty."

He dried her head gently and then kept the towel over her head and brought a hand blower and began to play it through her hair as he combed it forward.

"Now watch," he said.

As the air drove through her hair it was turning from damp drab to a silvery northern shining fairness. As the wind of the blower moved through it they watched it change.

"You shouldn't have despaired," Monsieur Jean said, not saying *Madame* and then remembering. "Madame wanted it fair?"

"It's better than the pearls," she said. "You're a great man and I was terrible."

Then he rubbed his hands together with something from a jar. "I'll just touch it with this," he said. He smiled at Catherine very happily and passed his hands lightly over her head.

Catherine stood up and looked at herself very seriously in the mirror. Her face had never been so dark and her hair was like the bark of a young white birch tree.

"I like it so much," she said. "Too much."

She looked in the mirror as though she had never seen the girl she was looking at.

"Now we must do Monsieur," the coiffeur said. "Does Monsieur wish the cut? It's very conservative but it's also sportif."

"The cut," David said. "I don't think I've had a haircut in a month."

"Please make it the same as mine," Catherine said.

"But shorter," David said.

"No. Please just the same."

When it was cut David stood up and ran his hand over his head. It felt cool and comfortable.

"Aren't you going to let him lighten it?"

"No. We've had enough miracles for one day."

"Just a little?"

"No."

David looked at Catherine and then at his own face in the mirror. His was as brown as hers and it was her haircut.

"You really want it that much?"

"Yes I do, David. Truly. Just to try it a little bit. Please."

He looked once more in the mirror and walked over then and sat down. The coiffeur looked at Catherine.

"Go ahead and do it," she said.

Chapter Ten

THE PATRON WAS SITTING at one of his tables on the terrace of the long house with a bottle of wine, a glass and an empty coffee cup reading the *Éclaireur de Nice* when the blue car came up in a rush on the gravel and Catherine and David got out and came walking down the flagstones to the terrace. He had not expected them back so soon and he was nearly asleep but he stood up and said the first thing that came in his head as they were opposite him.

"*Madame et Monsieur ont fait décolorer les cheveux. C'est bien.*"

"*Merci Monsieur. On le fait toujours dans le mois d'août.*"

"*C'est bien. C'est très bien.*"

"That's nice," said Catherine to David. "We're good clients. What the good client does is très bien. You're très bien. My God you are."

In their room a good sailing breeze was blowing in from the sea and the room was cold.

"I love that blue shirt," David said. "Stand there like that in it."

"It's the color of the car," she said. "Would it look nicer without a skirt?"

"Everything on you looks nicer without a skirt," he said. "I'm going out and see that old goat and be an even better client."

He came back with a bucket of ice and a bottle of the champagne that the proprietor had ordered for them and that they had drunk so seldom and he held two glasses on a small tray in his other hand.

"This ought to be fair warning for them," he said.

"We didn't need it," Catherine said.

"We can just try it. It won't take fifteen minutes to cool."

"Don't tease. Please come to bed and let me see you and feel you."

She was taking his shirt up over his head and he stood up and helped her.

After she was asleep David got up and looked at himself in the bathroom mirror. He picked up a brush and brushed his hair. There was no other way to brush it but the way it had been cut. It would disarrange and muss but it had to fall that way and the color was the same as Catherine's. He went to the door and looked at her on the bed. Then he came back and picked up her big hand mirror.

"So that's how it is," he said to himself. "You've done that to your hair and had it cut the same as your girl's and how do you feel?" He asked the mirror. "How do you feel? Say it."

"You like it," he said.

He looked at the mirror and it was someone else he saw but it was less strange now.

"All right. You like it," he said. "Now go through with the rest of it whatever it is and don't ever say anyone tempted you or that anyone bitched you."

He looked at the face that was no longer strange to him at all but was his face now and said, "You like it. Remember that. Keep that straight. You know exactly how you look now and how you are."

Of course he did not know exactly how he was. But he made an effort aided by what he had seen in the mirror.

They ate dinner on the terrace in front of the long house that night and were very excited and quiet and enjoyed looking at each other in the shaded light on the table. After dinner Catherine said to the boy who had brought their coffee, "Find the pail for the champagne in our room and ice a new bottle please."

"Do we want another?" David asked.

"I think so. Don't you?"

"Sure."

"You don't have to."

"Do you want a *fine?*"

"No. I'd rather drink the wine. Do you have to work tomorrow?"

"We'll see."

"Please work if you feel like it."

"And tonight?"

"We'll see about tonight. It's been such an arduous day."

In the night it was very dark and the wind had risen and they could hear it in the pines.

"David?"

"Yes."

"How are you girl?"

"I'm fine."

"Let me feel your hair girl. Who cut it? Was it Jean? It's cut so full and has so much body and it's the same as mine. Let me kiss you girl. Oh you have lovely lips. Shut your eyes girl."

He did not shut his eyes but it was dark in the room and outside the wind was high in the trees.

"You know it isn't so easy to be a girl if you're really one. If you really feel things."

"I know."

"Nobody knows. I tell you so when you're my girl. It's not that you're insatiable. I'm satiable so easily. It's just some feel and others don't. People lie about it I think. But it's so nice just to feel and hold you. I'm so happy. Just be my girl and love me the way I love you. Love me more. The way you can now. You now. Yes you. Please you."

They were dropping down the slope toward Cannes and the wind was heavy as they came onto the plain and skirted the deserted beaches, the tall grass bending and flattening as they crossed the bridge over the river and picked up speed on the last stretch of fast road before the town. David found the bottle, which was cold and wrapped in a towel, and took a long drink and felt the car leave the work behind and move away and up the small rise the black road was making. He had not worked this morning and now when she had driven them through the town and back into the country, he uncorked the bottle and drank again and offered it to her.

"I don't need it," Catherine said. "I feel too good."

"Very well."

They passed Golfe-Juan with the good bistro and the small open bar and then were through the pine woods and moving along the raw yellow beach of Juan-les-Pins. They crossed the small peninsula on the fast black road and passed through Antibes driving beside the railway and then out through the town and beyond the port and the square tower of the old defenses and came out again into open country. "It never lasts," she said. "I always eat that stretch too fast."

They stopped and ate lunch in the lee of an old stone wall that was part of the ruin of some building hard by the side of a clear stream that came out of the mountains and crossed the wild plain on its way to the sea. The wind came hard out of a funnel in the mountains. They had spread a blanket on the ground and they sat close together against the wall and looked out across the waste country to the sea that was flat and scoured by the wind.

"It wasn't much of a place to come to," Catherine said. "I don't know what I thought it would be like."

They stood up and looked up at the hills with their poised villages and the gray and purple mountains behind. The wind whipped in their hair and Catherine pointed out a road that she had once driven into the high country.

"We could have gone somewhere up in there," she said. "But it's so closed in and picturesque. I hate those hanging villages."

"This is a good place," David said. "It's a fine stream and we couldn't have a better wall."

"You're being nice. You don't have to be."

"It's a good lee and I like the place. We'll turn our back on all the picturesque."

They ate stuffed eggs, roast chicken, pickles, fresh long bread that they broke in pieces and spread Sovora mustard on and they drank rosé.

"Do you feel good now?" Catherine asked.

"Sure."

"And you haven't felt bad?"

"No."

"Not even about anything I said?"

David took a drink of the wine and said, "No. I haven't thought about it."

She stood up and looked into the wind so that it blew her sweater against her breasts and whipped her hair and then she looked down at him with her black brown face and smiled. She turned around then and looked out toward the sea that was flattened and wrinkled by the wind.

"Let's go get the papers in Cannes and read them in the cafe," she said.

"You want to show off."

"Why shouldn't I? It's the first time we've been out together. Do you mind if we do?"

"No, Devil. Why would I?"

"I didn't want to if you didn't."

"You said you wanted to."

"I want to do what you want. I can't be more compliant than that can I?"

"Nobody wants you to be compliant."

"Can we stop it? All I wanted to be was good today. Why spoil everything?"

"Let's clean up here and go."

"Where?"

"Anywhere. The god damn cafe."

They bought the papers in Cannes and a new French *Vogue*, the *Chasseur Français* and the *Miroir des Sports* and sat at a table in front of the cafe out of the wind and read and had their drinks and were friends again. David drank Haig pinch bottle and Perrier and Catherine had Armagnac and Perrier.

Two girls who had driven up and parked on the street came over to the cafe and sat down and ordered a Chambery Cassis and a *fine à l'eau.* It was the beauty of the two who took the brandy and soda.

"Who are those two?" Catherine said. "Do you know?"

"I've never seen them."

"I have. They must live around here somewhere. I saw them in Nice."

"The one girl's handsome," David said. "She has fine legs too."

"They're sisters," Catherine said. "They're both nice looking really."

"But the one's a beauty. They're not Americans."

The two girls were arguing and Catherine said to David, "It's a big row, I think."

"How did you know they were sisters?"

"I thought they were in Nice. Now I'm not sure. The car has Swiss plates."

"It's an old Isotta."

"Should we wait and see what happens? We haven't seen any drama for a long time."

"I think it's just a big Italian row."

"It must be getting serious because it's quieter."

"It will flare up. The one is a damned handsome girl."

"Yes, she is. And here she comes over."

David stood up.

"I'm sorry," the girl said in English. "Please forgive me. Please sit down," she said to David.

"Will you sit down?" Catherine asked.

"I shouldn't. My friend is furious with me. But I told her you would understand. You will forgive me?"

"Should we forgive her?" Catherine said to David.

"Let's forgive her."

"I knew you would understand," the girl said. "It's only to tell me where you had your hair cut." She blushed. "Or is it like copying a dress? My friend said it was more offensive."

"I'll write it down for you," Catherine said.

"I'm very ashamed," the girl said. "You're not offended?"

"Of course not," Catherine said. "Would you have a drink with us?"

"I shouldn't. May I ask my friend?"

She went back to her table for a moment and there was a short and vicious low-pitched exchange.

"My friend regrets very much but she cannot come over," the girl said. "But I hope we will meet again. You have been so very kind."

"How about that?" Catherine said when the girl had gone back to her friend. "For on a windy day."

"She'll be back to ask where you had your slacks cut."

The row was still going on at the other table. Then the two of them stood up and came over.

"May I present my friend the—"

"I am Nina."

"Our name is Bourne," David said. "How very pleasant of you to join us."

"You were very nice to let us come over," the handsome one said. "It was an impudent thing to do." She blushed.

"It's very flattering," Catherine said. "But he's a very good coiffeur."

"He must be," the handsome one said. She had a breathless way of speaking and she blushed again. "We saw you in Nice," she said to Catherine. "I wanted to speak to you then. I mean ask you."

She can't blush again, David thought. But she did.

"Who's going to have their hair cut?" Catherine asked.

"I am," the handsome one said.

"I am too, stupid," Nina said.

"You said you weren't."

"I changed my mind."

"I *really am,*" the handsome one said. "We must go now. Do you come here to this cafe?"

"Sometimes," Catherine said.

"I hope we'll see you sometime then," the handsome one said. "Goodbye and thank you for being so gracious."

The two girls went to their table and Nina called the waiter and they paid and were gone.

"They're not Italian," David said. "The one is nice but she could make you nervous blushing."

"She's in love with you."

"Sure. She saw *me* in Nice."

"Well I can't help it if she is with me. It isn't the first girl that ever was and a lot of good it did them."

"How about Nina?"

"That bitch," Catherine said.

"She was a wolf. I suppose it should be amusing."

"I didn't think it was amusing," Catherine said. "I thought it was sad."

"So did I."

"We'll find another cafe," she said. "They're gone now anyway."

"They were spooky."

"I know," she said. "For me too. But the one girl was nice. She had beautiful eyes. Did you see?"

"She was an awful blusher though."

"I liked her. Didn't you?"

"I suppose so."

"People that can't blush are worthless."

"Nina blushed once," David said.

"I could be awfully rude to Nina."

"It wouldn't touch her."

"No. She's well armored."

"Do you want another drink before we go home?"

"I don't need one. But you have one."

"I don't need one."

"Have another. You usually have two in the evening. I'll take a small one to keep company."

"No. Let's go home."

In the night he woke and heard the wind high and wild and turned and pulled the sheet over his shoulder and shut his eyes again. He felt her breathing and shut his eyes again. He felt her breathing softly and regularly and then he went back to sleep.

Chapter Eleven

IT WAS THE SECOND DAY of the wind and it had not slackened. He left the ongoing narrative of their journey where it was to write a story that had come to him four or five days before and had been developing, probably, he thought, in the last two nights while he had slept. He knew it was bad to interrupt any work he was engaged in but he felt confident and sure of how well he was going and he thought he could leave the longer narrative and write the story which he believed he must write now or lose.

The story started with no difficulty as a story does when it is ready to be written and he got past the middle of it and knew he should break off and leave it until the next day. If he could not keep away from it after he had taken a break he would drive through and finish it. But he hoped he could keep away from it and hit it fresh the next day. It was a good story and now he remembered how long he had intended to write it. The story had not come to him in the past few days. His memory had been inaccurate in that. It was the necessity to write it that had come to him. He knew how the story ended now. He had always known the wind and sand-scoured bones but they were gone now and he was inventing all of it. It was all true now because it happened to him as he wrote and only its bones were dead and scattered and behind him. It started now with the evil in the shamba and he had to write it and he was very well into it.

He was tired and happy from his work when he found Catherine's note that she had not wanted to disturb him, had gone out and would be back for lunch. He left the room and ordered breakfast and, as he waited for it, Monsieur Aurol, the proprietor, came in and they spoke about the weather. Monsieur Aurol said the wind came this way sometimes. It was not a true mistral, the season guaranteed that, but it would probably blow for three days. The weather was insane now. Monsieur had undoubtedly noticed that. If anyone kept track of it they would know that it had not been normal since the war.

David said he had not been able to keep track of it because he had been travelling but there was no doubt that the weather was strange. Not only the weather, said Monsieur Aurol, everything was changed and what was not changed was changing fast. It might very well all be for the best and he, for one, did not oppose it. Monsieur, as a man of the world, probably saw it in the same way.

Undoubtedly, said David, seeking for a decisive and terminal idiocy, it was necessary to review the *cadres*.

Precisely, said Monsieur Aurol.

They left it at that and David finished his café crème and read the *Miroir des Sports* and began to miss Catherine. He went into the room and found *Far Away and Long Ago* and came out onto the terrace and settled himself in the sun by the table out of the wind to read the lovely book. Catherine had sent to Galignani's in Paris for the Dent edition for a present for him and when the books had come they had made him feel truly rich. The figures in his bank balances, the franc and dollar accounts, had, ever since

Grau du Roi, seemed completely unreal and he had never considered them as actual money. But the books of W. H. Hudson had made him feel rich and when he told Catherine this she was very pleased.

After he had read an hour he started to miss Catherine very badly and he found the boy who served at table and asked him to bring a whiskey and Perrier. Later he had another. It was well past lunch when he heard the car come up the hill.

They came along the walk and he heard their voices. They were excited and happy, then the girl was suddenly silent, and Catherine said, "Look who I brought to see you."

"Please, I know I should not have come," the girl said. It was the dark handsome one of the two they had met at the cafe yesterday; the one who blushed.

"How are you?" David said. She had evidently been to the coiffeur's and her hair had been cropped short the way Catherine's had been at Biarritz. "I see you found the place."

The girl blushed and looked at Catherine for courage.

"Look at her," Catherine said. "Go muss her head up."

"Oh Catherine," the girl said. Then she said to David, "You can if you want."

"Don't be frightened," he said. "What do you think you've got into?"

"I don't know," she said. "I'm just so happy to be here."

"Where have you two been?" David asked Catherine.

"Jean's of course. Then we just stopped and had a drink and I asked Marita if she'd come to lunch. Aren't you glad to see us?"

"I'm delighted. Will you have another drink?"

"Would you make martinis?" Catherine asked. "One won't hurt you," she said to the girl.

"No please. I have to drive."

"Do you want a sherry?"

"No please."

David went behind the bar and found glasses and some ice and made two martinis.

"I'll taste yours if I may," the girl said to him.

"You're not afraid of him now are you?" Catherine asked her.

"Not at all," the girl said. She blushed again. "It tastes very good but terribly strong."

"They are strong," David said. "But there's a strong wind today and we drink according to the wind."

"Oh," said the girl. "Do all Americans do that?"

"Only the oldest families," Catherine said. "Us, the Morgans, the Woolworths, the Jelkses, the Jukeses. You know."

"It's rugged in the blizzards and in hurricane months," David said. "Sometimes I wonder if we'll get through the autumnal equinox."

"I'd like to have one sometime when I didn't have to drive," the girl said.

"You don't have to drink because we do," Catherine said. "And don't mind that we make jokes all the time. Look at her David. Aren't you glad I brought her?"

"I love it that you make jokes," the girl said. "You must forgive me that I'm so happy to be here."

"You were nice to come," David said.

When they were at lunch in the dining room out of the wind, David asked, "What about your friend Nina?"

"She's gone away."

"She was handsome," David said.

"Yes. We had a very big fight and she went away."

"She was a bitch," Catherine said. "But then I think almost everyone is a bitch."

"Usually they are," the girl said. "I always hope not but they are."

"I know plenty of women who aren't bitches," David said.

"Yes. You would," the girl said.

"Was Nina happy?" Catherine asked.

"I hope she will be happy," the girl said. "Happiness in intelligent people is the rarest thing I know."

"You haven't had such a long time to find out about it."

"If you make mistakes you find out faster," the girl said.

"You've been happy all morning," Catherine said. "We had a wonderful time."

"You don't need to tell me," the girl said. "And I'm happier now than I can remember ever."

Later, over salad David asked the girl, "Are you staying far from here along the coast?"

"I don't think I'm staying."

"Really? That's too bad," he said and felt the tension come to the table and draw taut as a hawser. He looked from the girl with her eyelashes down so they touched her cheeks to Catherine and she looked at him very straight and said, "She was going back to Paris and I said why not stay here if Aurol has a room? Come on up to lunch and see if David likes you and if you like the place. David do you like her?"

"It's not a club," David said. "It's a hotel." Catherine looked away and he moved fast to help her, going on as though it had not been stated. "We like you very much and I'm sure Aurol has room. He should be delighted to have someone else here."

The girl sat at the table with her eyes down. "I think I'd better not."

"Please stay a few days," Catherine said. "David and I would both love to have you. I've no one here to keep me company while he works. We'd have good times the way we did this morning. Tell her David."

The hell with her, David thought. Fuck her.

"Don't be silly," he said. "Call Monsieur Aurol please," he told the boy who served. "We'll find out about a room."

"You won't mind truly?" the girl asked.

"We wouldn't have asked you if we minded," David said. "We like you and you're very decorative."

"I'll be useful if I can," the girl said. "I hope I'll find out how to be."

"Be happy the way you were when you came in," David told her. "That's useful."

"I am now," the girl said. "I wish I'd taken the martini now that I don't have to drive."

"You can have one tonight," Catherine said.

"That will be lovely. Can we go and see the rooms now and get it over with?"

David had driven her down to retrieve the big old Isotta convertible and her bags from where the car had been parked in front of the cafe in Cannes.

On the way she said, "Your wife is wonderful and I'm in love with her."

She was sitting beside him and David did not look to see if she blushed.

"I'm in love with her too," he said.

"I'm in love with you also," she said. "Is that all right?"

He dropped his arm and closed his hand on her shoulder and she leaned close against him.

"We'll have to see about that," he said.

"I'm glad I'm smaller."

"Smaller than who?"

"Catherine," she said.

"That's a hell of a thing to say," he said.

"I mean I thought you might like someone of my size. Or do you only care for tall girls?"

"Catherine's not a tall girl."

"Of course not. I only meant that I was not as tall."

"Yes and you're very dark too."

"Yes. We'll look well together."

"Who will?"

"Catherine and I and you and I."

"We'll have to."

"What does that mean?"

"I mean we can't escape looking well together can we, if we look well and we are together?"

"We're together now."

"No." He was driving with only one hand on the wheel, leaning back and looking up the road ahead at the juncture with the N.7. She had put her hand on him. "We're just riding in the same car," he said.

"But I can feel that you like me."

"Yes. I'm very reliable that way but it doesn't mean a thing."

"It does mean something."

"Just what it says."

"It's a very nice thing to say," she said and did not say anything more nor take her hand away until they had turned at the Boulevard and pulled up behind the old Isotta Fraschini parked in front of the cafe under the old trees. Then she had smiled at him and got out of the small blue car.

Now, at the hotel in the pines that were still being blown by the wind, David and Catherine were alone in their room after she finally came in from settling the girl in the two rooms that she had taken.

"I think she'll be comfortable," Catherine said. "Of course the best room beside our own is the one at the far end where you work."

"And I'm going to keep it," David said. "I'm going damn well and I won't change my work room for an imported bitch!"

"Why are you being so violent?" Catherine said. "No one asked you to give it up. I just said it was the best. But the two next door to it work out very well."

"Who is this girl anyway?"

"Don't be so violent. She's a nice girl and I like her. I know it was unforgivable to bring her up without speaking to you and I'm sorry. But I did it and it's done. I thought you'd like to have someone pleasant and attractive for me to have as a friend to go around with while you're working."

"I do if you want someone."

"I didn't *want* someone. I just ran into someone that I liked and thought you would like and it would be pleasant for her to be here for a little while."

"But who is she?"

"I haven't examined her papers. You interrogate her if you need to."

"Well, she's decorative at least. But whose girl is she?"

"Don't be rough. She's nobody's."

"Tell me straight."

"All right. She's in love with us both unless I'm crazy."

"You're not crazy."

"Not yet maybe."

"So what's the drill?"

"I wouldn't know," Catherine said.

"I wouldn't either."

"It's sort of strange and fun."

"I wouldn't know," David said. "Do you want to go to swim? We missed it yesterday."

"Let's swim. Should we ask her? It would only be polite."

"We'd have to wear suits."

"It wouldn't matter with this wind. It's no day to be on the sand to tan."

"I hate to wear suits with you."

"Me too. But maybe tomorrow the wind will be over."

Then on the Estérel road with David driving the big old Isotta, feeling and condemning the too sudden brakes and finding how badly the motor needed to be worked over, the three of them sat together and Catherine said, "There are two or three different coves where we swim without suits when we're alone. That's the only way to get really dark."

"It's not a good day to tan," David said. "It's too windy."

"We can swim though without suits if you like," Catherine said to the girl. "If David doesn't mind. It might be fun."

"I'd love to," the girl said. "Do you mind?" she asked David.

In the evening David made martinis and the girl said, "Is everything always as wonderful as it has been today?"

"It's been a pleasant day," David said. Catherine had not yet come out from their room and he and the girl were sitting in front of the small bar M. Aurol had installed the previous winter in the corner of the big Provençal room.

"When I drink I want to say things I should never say," the girl said.

"Then don't say them."

"Then what's the use of drinking?"

"It isn't these. You've only had one."

"Were you embarrassed when we swam?"

"No. Should I have been?"

"No," she said. "I loved to see you."

"That's good," he said. "How's the martini?"

"It's very strong but I like it. Did you and Catherine never swim before like that with anyone?"

"No. Why should we?"

"I'll get really brown."

"I'm sure you will."

"Would you rather I was not so deeply brown?"

"You're a nice color. Get that color all over if you like."

"I thought perhaps you'd like one of your girls lighter than the other."

"You're not my girl."

"I am," she said. "I told you before."

"You don't blush anymore."

"I got over it when we went bathing. I hope I won't now for a long time. That's why I said everything—to get over it. That's why I told you."

"You look nice in that cashmere sweater," David said.

"Catherine said we'd both wear them. You don't dislike me because I told you?"

"I forget what you told me."

"That I love you."

"Don't talk rot."

"Don't you believe it happens to people like that? The way it happened to me about you two?"

"You don't fall in love with two people at once."

"You don't know," she said.

"It's rot," he said. "It's just a way of talking."

"It isn't at all. It's true."

"You just think it is. It's nonsense."

"All right," she said. "It's nonsense. But I'm here."

"Yes. You're here," he said. He was watching Catherine as she crossed the room, smiling and happy.

"Hello swimmers," she said. "Oh what a shame. I didn't get to see Marita have her first martini."

"This is still it," the girl said.

"How did it affect her, David?"

"Made her talk rot."

"We'll start with a fresh one. Weren't you good to resuscitate this bar. It's such a sort of tentative bar. We'll get a mirror for it. A bar's no good without a mirror."

"We can get one tomorrow," the girl said. "I'd like to get it."

"Don't be rich," Catherine said. "We'll both get it and then we can all see each other when we talk rot and know how rotty it is. You can't fool a bar mirror."

"It's when I start looking quizzical in one that I know I've lost," David said.

"You never lose. How can you lose with two girls?" Catherine said.

"I tried to tell him," the girl said and blushed for the first time that evening.

"She's your girl and I'm your girl," Catherine said. "Now stop being stuffy and be nice to your girls. Don't you like the way they look? I'm the very fair one you married."

"You're darker and fairer than the one I married."

"So are you and I brought you a dark girl for a present. Don't you like your present?"

"I like my present very much."

"How do you like your future?"

"I don't know about my future."

"It isn't a dark future is it?" the girl asked.

"Very good," Catherine said. "She's not only beautiful and rich and healthy and affectionate. She can make jokes. Aren't you pleased with what I brought you?"

"I'd rather be a dark present than a dark future," the girl said.

"She did it again," Catherine said. "Give her a kiss David and make her a fair present."

David put his arm around the girl and kissed her and she started to kiss him and turned her head away. Then she was crying with her head down and both hands holding the bar.

"Make a good joke now," David said to Catherine.

"I'm all right," the girl said. "Don't look at me. I'm all right."

Catherine put her arm around her and kissed her and stroked her head.

"I'll be all right," the girl said. "Please, I know I'll be all right."

"I'm so sorry," Catherine said.

"Let me go please," the girl said. "I have to go."

"Well," David said when the girl was gone and Catherine had come back to the bar.

"You don't need to say it," Catherine said. "I'm sorry David."

"She'll be back."

"You don't think it's all a fake now do you?"

"They were real tears if that's what you mean."

"Don't be stupid. You aren't stupid."

"I kissed her very carefully."

"Yes. On the mouth."

"Where did you expect me to kiss her?"

"You were all right. I haven't criticized you."

"I'm glad you didn't ask me to kiss her when we were at the beach."

"I thought of it," Catherine said. She laughed and it was like the old days before anyone had mixed in their life. "Did you think I was going to?"

"I thought you were so I dove in."

"Good thing you did."

They laughed again.

"Well, we've cheered up," Catherine said.

"Thank God," David said. "I love you, Devil, and really I didn't kiss her to make all that."

"You don't have to tell me," Catherine said. "I saw you. It was a miserable effort."

"I wish she'd go away."

"Don't be heartless," Catherine said. "And I did encourage her."

"I tried not to."

"I egged her on about you. I'll go out and find her."

"No. Wait a little while. She's too sure of herself."

"How can you say that, David? You just broke her all up."

"I did not."

"Well something did. I'm going to go and get her."

But it wasn't necessary because the girl came back to the bar where they were standing and blushed and said, "I'm sorry." Her face was washed and she had brushed her hair and she came up to David and kissed him on the mouth very quickly and said, "I like my present. Did someone take my drink?"

"I threw it out," Catherine said. "David will make a new one."

"I hope you still like having two girls," she said. "Because I am yours and I'm going to be Catherine's too."

"I don't go in for girls," Catherine said. It was very quiet and her voice did not sound right either to herself or to David.

"Don't you ever?"

"I never have."

"I can be your girl, if you ever want one, and David's too."

"Don't you think that's sort of a vast undertaking?" Catherine asked.

"That's why I came here," the girl said. "I thought that was what you wanted."

"I've never had a girl," Catherine said.

"I'm so stupid," the girl said. "I didn't know. Is it true? You're not making fun of me?"

"I'm not making fun of you."

"I don't know how I could be so stupid," the girl said. She means *mistaken* David thought and Catherine thought it too.

That night in bed Catherine said, "I never should have let you in for any of it. Not for any part of it."

"I wish we'd never seen her."

"It might have been something worse. Maybe to go through with it and get rid of it that way is best."

"You could send her away."

"I don't think that's the way to clear it now. Doesn't she do anything to you?"

"Oh sure."

"I knew she did. But I love you and all this is nothing. You know it is too."

"I don't know about it, Devil."

"Well we won't be solemn. I can already tell it's death if you're solemn."

Chapter Twelve

IT WAS THE THIRD DAY of the wind but it was not as heavy now and he sat at the table and read the story over from the start to where he had left off, correcting as he read. He went on with the story, living in it and nowhere else, and when he heard the voices of the two girls outside he did not listen. When they went by the window he lifted his hand and waved. They waved and the dark girl smiled and Catherine put her fingers to her lips. The girl looked very pretty in the morning, her face shining and her color high. Catherine was beautiful as always. He heard the car start and noted it was the Bugatti. He went back into the story. It was a good story and he finished it shortly before noon.

It was too late to have breakfast and he was tired after working and did not want to drive the old Isotta into town with its bad brakes and huge malfunctioning motor although the key was with a note Catherine had left saying they had gone to Nice and would look in at the cafe for him on their way home.

What I would like, he thought, is a tall cold liter of beer in a thick heavy glass and a *pomme à l'huile* with coarse ground peppercorns on it. But the beer on this coast was worthless and he thought happily of Paris and other places he had been and was pleased he had written something he knew was good and that he had finished it. This was the first writing he had finished since they were married. Finishing is what you have to do, he thought. If you don't finish, nothing is worth a damn. Tomorrow I'll pick up the narrative where I left it and keep right on until I finish it. And how are you going to finish it? How are you going to finish it now?

As soon as he started to think beyond his work, everything that he had locked out by the work came back to him. He thought of the night before and of Catherine and the girl today on the road that he and Catherine had driven two days before and he felt sick. They should be on the way back now. It's afternoon. Maybe they're at the cafe. Don't be solemn, she had said. But she meant something else too. Maybe she knows what she's doing. Maybe she knows how it can turn out. Maybe she does know. You don't.

So you worked and now you worry. You'd better write another story. Write the hardest one there is to write that you know. Go ahead and do that. You have to last yourself if you're to be any good to her. What good have you been to her? Plenty, he said. No, not plenty. Plenty means enough. Go ahead and start the new one tomorrow. The hell with tomorrow. What a way to be. *Tomorrow.* Go in and start it now.

He put the note and the key in his pocket and went back into the work room and sat down and wrote the first paragraph of the new story that he had always put off writing since he had known what a story was. He wrote it in simple declarative sentences with all of the problems ahead to be lived through and made to come alive. The very beginning was written and all he had to do was go on. That's all, he said. You see how simple what you cannot do is? Then he came out onto the terrace and sat down and ordered a whiskey and Perrier.

The proprietor's young nephew brought the bottles and ice and a glass from the bar and said, "Monsieur had no breakfast."

"I worked too long."

"*C'est dommage,*" the boy said. "Can I bring anything? A sandwich?"

"In our storeroom you will find a tin of Maquereau Vin Blanc Capitaine Cook. Open it up and bring me two on a plate."

"They won't be cold."

"It makes no difference. Bring them."

He sat and ate the maquereau vin blanc and drank the whiskey and mineral water. It did make a difference that they were not cold. He read the morning paper while he ate.

We always ate fresh fish at le Grau du Roi, he thought, but that was a long time ago. He started to remember Grau du Roi and then he heard the car coming up the hill.

"Take this away," he said to the boy and he stood up and walked into the bar and poured himself a whiskey, put ice in it and filled the glass with Perrier. The taste of the wine-spiced fish was in his mouth and he picked up the bottle of mineral water and drank from it.

He heard their voices and then they came in the door as happy and gay as yesterday. He saw Catherine's birch bright head and her dark face loving and excited and the other girl dark, the wind still in her hair, her eyes very bright and then suddenly shy again as she came closer.

"We didn't stop when we saw you weren't at the cafe," Catherine said.

"I worked late. How are you, Devil?"

"I'm very well. Don't ask me how this one is."

"Did you work well, David?" the girl asked.

"That's being a good wife," Catherine said. "I forgot to ask."

"What did you do in Nice?"

"Can we have a drink and then tell?"

They were close to him on each side and he felt them both.

"Did you work well, David?" she asked again.

"Of course he did," Catherine said. "That's the only way he ever works, stupid."

"Did you, David?"

"Yes," he said and rumpled her head. "Thanks."

"Don't we get a drink?" Catherine asked. "We didn't work at all. We just bought things and ordered things and made scandal."

"We didn't make any real scandal."

"I don't know," Catherine said. "I don't care either."

"What was the scandal?" David asked.

"It wasn't anything," the girl said.

"I didn't mind it," Catherine said. "I liked it."

"Someone said something about her slacks in Nice."

"That's not a scandal," David said. "It's a big town. You had to expect that if you went there."

"Do I look any different?" Catherine asked. "I wish they'd brought the mirror. Do I look any different to you?"

"No." David looked at her. She looked very blond and disheveled and darker than ever and very excited and defiant.

"That's good," she said. "Because I tried it."

"You didn't do anything," the girl said.

"I did and I liked it and I want another drink."

"She didn't do anything, David," the girl said.

"This morning I stopped the car on the long clear stretch and kissed her and she kissed me and on the way back from Nice too and when we got out of the car just now." Catherine looked at him lovingly but rebelliously and then said, "It was fun and I liked it. You kiss her too. The boy's not here."

David turned to the girl and she clung to him suddenly and they kissed. He had not meant to kiss her and he had not known it would be like this when he did it.

"That's enough," Catherine said.

"How are you?" David said to the girl. She was shy and happy again.

"I'm happy the way you said to be," the girl told him.

"Everybody is happy now," Catherine said. "We've shared all the guilt."

They had a very good lunch and drank cold Tavel through the hors d'oeuvres, the poulet and the ratatouille, the salad and the fruit and cheese. They were all hungry and they made jokes and no one was solemn.

"There's a terrific surprise for dinner or before," Catherine said. "She spends money like a drunken oil-lease Indian, David."

"Are they nice?" the girl asked. "Or are they like Maharajas?"

"David will tell you about them. He comes from Oklahoma."

"I thought he came from East Africa."

"No. Some of his ancestors escaped from Oklahoma and took him to East Africa when he was very young."

"It must have been very exciting."

"He wrote a novel about being in East Africa when he was a boy."

"I know."

"You read it?" David asked her.

"I did," she said. "Do you want to ask me about it?"

"No," he said. "I'm familiar with it."

"It made me cry," the girl said. "Was that your father in it?"

"Some ways."

"You must have loved him very much."

"I did."

"You never talked to me about him," Catherine said.

"You never asked me."

"Would you have?"

"No," he said.

"I loved the book," the girl said.

"Don't overreach," Catherine said.

"I wasn't."

"When you kissed him—"

"You asked me to."

"What I wanted to say when you interrupted," Catherine said, "was did you think of him as a writer when you kissed him and liked it so much?"

David poured a glass of Tavel and drank some of it.

"I don't know," the girl said. "I didn't think."

"I'm glad," Catherine said. "I was afraid it was going to be like the clippings."

The girl looked really mystified and Catherine explained, "The press cuttings about the second book. He's written two you know."

"I only read *The Rift*."

"The second one is about flying. In the war. It's the only good thing anyone ever wrote about flying."

"Balls," David said.

"Wait until you read it," Catherine said. "It's a book you had to die to write and you had to be completely destroyed. Don't ever think I don't know about his books just because I don't think he's a writer when I kiss him."

"I think we ought to take a siesta," David said. "You ought to take a nap, Devil. You're tired."

"I talked too much," Catherine said. "It was a nice lunch and I'm sorry if I talked too much and boasted."

"I loved you when you talked about the books," the girl said. "You were admirable."

"I don't feel admirable. I am tired," Catherine said. "Have you plenty to read, Marita?"

"I have two books still," the girl said. "Later I'll borrow some if I may."

"May I come in to see you later?"

"If you want," the girl said.

David did not look at the girl and she did not look at him.

"I won't disturb you?" Catherine said.

"Nothing that I do is important," the girl said.

. . .

Catherine and David lay side by side on the bed in their room with the wind blowing its last day outside and it was not like siesta in the old days.

"Can I tell you now?"

"I'd rather skip it."

"No, let me tell. This morning when I started the car I was frightened and I tried to drive very well and I felt hollow inside. Then I could see Cannes up ahead on the hill and the road was clear all up ahead by the sea and I looked behind and it was clear and I pulled out from the road into the brush. Where it's like the sagebrush. I kissed her and she kissed me and we sat in the car and I felt very strange and then we drove into Nice and I don't know whether people could tell it or not. I didn't care by then and we went everywhere and bought everything. She loves to buy things. Someone made a rude remark but it was nothing really. Then we stopped on the way home and she said it was better if I was her girl and I said I didn't care either way and really I was glad because I am a girl now anyway and I didn't know what to do. I never felt so not knowing ever. But she's nice and she wanted to help me I think. I don't know. Anyway she was nice and I was driving and she was so pretty and happy and she was just gentle the way we are sometimes or me to you or either of us and I said I couldn't drive if she did that so we stopped. I only kissed her but I know it happened with me. So we were there for a while and then I drove straight home. I kissed her before we came in and we were happy and I liked it and I still like it."

"So now you've done it," David said carefully, "and you're through with it."

"But I'm not. I liked it and I'm going to really do it."

"No. You don't have to."

"I do and I'm going to do it until I'm through with it and I'm over it."

"Who says you'll be over it?"

"I do. But I really have to, David. I didn't know I'd ever be like this."

He did not say anything.

"I'll be back," she said. "I know I'll get over it as well as I know anything. Please trust me."

He did not say anything.

"She's waiting for me. Didn't you hear me ask her? It's like stopping in the middle of anything."

"I'm going up to Paris," David said. "You can reach me through the bank."

"No," she said. "No. You have to help me."

"I can't help you."

"You can. You can't go away. I couldn't stand it if you went away. I don't want to be with her. It's only something that I have to do. Can't you understand? Please understand. You always understand."

"Not this part."

"Please try. You always understood before. You know you did. Everything. Didn't you?"

"Yes. Before."

"It started with us and there'll only be us when I get this finished. I'm not in love with anyone else."

"Don't do it."

"I have to. Ever since I went to school all I ever had was chances to do it and people wanting to do it with me. And I never would and never did. But now I have to."

He said nothing.

"Please know how it is."

He did not say anything.

"Anyway she's in love with you and you can have her and wash everything away that way."

"You're talking crazy, Devil."

"I know it," she said. "I'll stop."

"Take a nap," he said. "Just lie close and quiet and we'll both go to sleep."

"I love you so," she said. "And you're my true partner the way I told her. I've told her too much about you but that's all she likes to talk about. I'm quiet now so I'm going to go."

"No. Don't."

"Yes," she said. "You wait for me. I won't be very long."

When she came back to the room David was not there and she stood a long time and looked at the bed and then went to the bathroom door and opened it and stood and looked in the long mirror. Her face had no expression and she looked at herself from her head down to her feet with no expression on her face at all. The light was nearly gone when she went into the bathroom and shut the door behind her.

Chapter Thirteen

DAVID DROVE UP from Cannes in the dusk. The wind had fallen and he left the car in the usual place and walked up the path to where the light came out onto the patio and the garden. Marita came out of the doorway and walked toward him.

"Catherine feels terribly," she said. "Please be kind to her."

"The hell with both of you," David said.

"With me, yes. But not with her. You mustn't, David."

"Don't tell me what I must and what I mustn't."

"Don't you want to take care of her?"

"Not particularly."

"I do."

"You certainly have."

"Don't be a fool," she said. "You're not a fool. I tell you this is serious."

"Where is she?"

"In there waiting for you."

David went in the door. Catherine was sitting at the empty bar.

"Hello," she said. "They didn't bring the mirror."

"Hello, Devil," he said. "I'm sorry I was late."

He was shocked at the dead way she looked and at her toneless voice.

"I thought you'd gone away," she said.

"Didn't you see I hadn't taken anything?"

"I didn't look. You wouldn't need to take anything to go away."

"No," David said. "I just went into town."

"Oh," she said and looked at the wall.

"The wind's dropping," he said. "It will be a good day tomorrow."

"I don't care about tomorrow."

"Sure you do."

"No I don't. Don't ask me to."

"I won't ask you to," he said. "Have you had a drink?"

"No."

"I'll make one."

"It won't do any good."

"It might. We're still us." He was making the drink and she watched him mechanically as he stirred and then poured into the glasses.

"Put in the garlic olive," she said.

He handed her one of the glasses and lifted his and touched it against hers. "Here's to us."

She poured her glass out on the bar and looked at it flow along the wood. Then she picked up the olive and put it in her mouth. "There isn't any us," she said. "Not anymore."

David took a handkerchief out of his pocket and wiped the bar and made another drink.

"It's all shit," Catherine said. David handed her the drink and she looked at it and then poured it on the bar. David mopped it up again and wrung out his handkerchief. Then he drank his own martini and made two more.

"This one you drink," he said. "Just drink it."

"Just drink," she said. She lifted the glass and said, "Here's to you and your god damned handkerchief."

She drank the glass off and then held it, looking at it, and David was sure that she was going to throw it in his face. Then she put it down and picked the garlic olive out of it and ate it very carefully and handed David the pit.

"Semi-precious stone," she said. "Put it in your pocket. I'll have another one if you'll make it."

"But drink this one slowly."

"Oh I'm quite all right now," Catherine said. "You probably won't notice the difference. I'm sure it happens to everybody."

"Do you feel better?"

"Much better really. You just lose something and it's gone that's all. All we lose was all that we had. But we get some more. There's no problem is there?"

"Are you hungry?"

"No. But I'm sure everything will be all right. You said it would didn't you?"

"Of course it will."

"I wish I could remember what it was we lost. But it doesn't matter does it? You said it didn't matter."

"No."

"Then let's be cheerful. It's just gone whatever it was."

"It must have been something we forgot," he said. "We'll find it."

"I did something I know. But it's gone now."

"That's good."

"It wasn't anyone else's fault whatever it was."

"Don't talk about faults."

"I know what it was now," she smiled. "But I wasn't unfaithful. Really David. How could I be? I couldn't be. You know that. How could you say I was? Why did you say it?"

"You weren't."

"Of course I wasn't. I wish you hadn't said it though."

"I didn't say it, Devil."

"Somebody did. But I wasn't. I just did what I said I'd do. Where's Marita?"

"She's in her room I think."

"I'm glad I'm all right again. Once you took it back I was all right. I wish it was you had done it so I could take it back about you. We're us again aren't we? I didn't kill it."

"No."

She smiled again. "That's good. I'll go and get her. Do you mind? She was worried about me. Before you came back."

"She was?"

"I talked a lot," Catherine said. "I always talk too much. She's awfully nice, David, if you knew her. She was very good to me."

"The hell with her."

"No. You took all that back. Remember? I don't want to have all that again. Do you? It's too confusing. Truly."

"All right bring her. She'll be glad to see you're feeling good again."

"I know she will and you must make her feel good too."

"Sure. Does she feel badly?"

"Only when I did. When I knew I was unfaithful. I never was before you know. You go and bring her, David. Then she won't feel bad. No don't bother, I'll go."

Catherine went out the door and David watched her go. Her movements were less mechanical and her voice was better. When she came back she was smiling and her voice was almost natural.

"She's coming in just a minute," she said. "She's lovely, David. I'm so glad you brought her."

The girl came in and David said, "We were waiting for you."

She looked at him and looked away. Then she looked back at him and held herself very straight and said, "I'm sorry to be late."

"You look very handsome," David said and it was quite true but she had the saddest eyes he had ever seen.

"Make her a drink please, David. I had two," Catherine said to the girl.

"I'm glad you feel better," the girl said.

"David made me feel good again," Catherine said. "I told him all about everything and how lovely it was and he understands perfectly. He really approves."

The girl looked at David and he saw the way her teeth bit her upper lip and what she said to him with her eyes. "It was dull in town. I missed the swimming," he said.

"You don't know what you missed," Catherine said. "You missed everything. It was what I wanted to do all my life and now I've done it and I loved it."

The girl was looking down at her glass.

"The most wonderful thing is that I feel so grown up now. But it's exhausting. Of course it's what I wanted and now I've done it and I know I'm just an apprentice but I won't always be."

"Apprentice allowance claimed," David said and took a chance then and said very cheerfully, "Don't you ever talk on any other subjects? Perversion's dull and old fashioned. I didn't know people like us even kept up on it."

"I suppose it's only really interesting the first time one does it," Catherine said.

"And then only to the person who does it and a bloody bore to everyone else," David said. "Do you agree, Heiress?"

"Do you call her Heiress?" Catherine asked. "That's a nice funny name."

"I can't very well call her Ma'am or Highness," David said. "Do you agree, Heiress? About perversion?"

"I always thought it was overrated and silly," she said. "It's only something girls do because they have nothing better."

"But one's first time at anything is interesting," Catherine said.

"Yes," David said. "But would you want to always talk about your first ride at Steeplechase Park or how you, yourself, personally soloed alone all by yourself in a plane absolutely away from the earth and up in the sky?"

"I'm ashamed," Catherine said. "Look at me and see if I'm not ashamed."

David put his arm around her.

"Don't be ashamed," he said. "Just remember how you'd like to hear old Heiress here recall how she went up in that plane, just herself and the plane, and there was nothing between her and the earth, imagine the Earth, with a big E, but just her *plane* and they might have been *killed* and smashed to horrible *bits* both of them and she lose her money and her health and her sanity and her life with a capital L and her loved ones or me or you or Jesus, all with capital letters, if she "crashed"—put the word *crashed* in quotes."

"Did you ever solo, Heiress?"

"No," the girl said. "I don't have to now. But I would like another drink. I love you, David."

"Kiss her again the way you did before," Catherine said.

"Sometime," David said. "I'm making drinks."

"I'm so glad we're all friends again and everything is fine," Catherine said. She was very animated now and her voice was natural and almost relaxed.

"I forgot about the surprise that Heiress bought this morning. I'll go and get it."

When Catherine was gone, the girl took David's hand and held it very tight and then kissed it. They sat and looked at each other. She touched his hand with her fingers almost absentmindedly. She curled her fingers around his and then released them. "We don't need to talk," she said. "You don't want me to make a speech do you?"

"No. But we have to talk sometime."

"Would you like me to go away?"

"You'd be smarter to go away."

"Would you kiss me so I know that it is all right if I stay?"

Catherine had come in now with the young waiter who carried a large tin of caviar in a bowl of ice on a tray with a plate of toast. "That was a wonderful kiss," she said. "Everyone saw it so there's no longer any fear of scandal or anything," Catherine said. "They're cutting up some egg whites and some onion."

It was very large firm gray caviar and Catherine dipped it onto the pieces of thin toast.

"Heiress bought you a case of Bollinger Brut 1915 and there is some iced. Don't you think we should drink a bottle with this?"

"Sure," said David. "Let's have it all through the meal."

"Isn't it lucky Heiress and I are rich so you'll never have anything to worry about? We'll take good care of him won't we Heiress?"

"We must try very hard," the girl said. "I'm trying to study his needs. This was all we could find for today."

Chapter Fourteen

HE HAD SLEPT about two hours when the daylight woke him and he looked at Catherine sleeping easily and looking happy in her sleep. He left her looking beautiful and young and unspoiled and then went into the bathroom and showered and put on a pair of shorts and walked barefoot through the garden to the room where he worked. The sky was washed clean after the wind and it was the fresh early morning of a new day toward the end of summer.

He started in again on the new and difficult story and worked attacking each thing that for years he had put off facing. He worked until nearly eleven o'clock and when he had finished for the day he shut up the room and went out and found the two girls playing chess at a table in the garden. They both looked fresh and young and as attractive as the wind-washed morning sky.

"She's beating me again," Catherine said. "How are you, David?"

The girl smiled at him very shyly.

They are the two loveliest girls I've ever seen, David thought. Now what will this day bring. "How are you two?" he said.

"We're very well," the girl said. "Did you have good luck?"

"It's all uphill but it's going well," he said.

"You haven't had any breakfast."

"It's too late for breakfast," David said.

"Nonsense," Catherine said. "You're wife of the day, Heiress. Make him eat breakfast."

"Wouldn't you like coffee and some fruit, David?" the girl asked. "You ought to eat something."

"I'll have some black coffee," David said.

"I'll bring you something," the girl said and went off into the hotel.

David sat by Catherine at the table and she put the chessmen and the board on a chair. She mussed his hair and said, "Have you forgotten you have a silver head like mine?"

"Yes," he said.

"It's going to be lighter and lighter and I'll be fairer and fairer and darker in the body too."

"That will be wonderful."

"Yes and I'm all over everything."

The pretty dark girl was bringing a tray with a small bowl rounded with caviar, a half lemon, a spoon and two pieces of toast and the young waiter had a bucket with a bottle of the Bollinger and a tray with three glasses.

"This will be good for David," the girl said. "Then we can go swimming before lunch."

After the swimming and lying in the sun on the beach and a big long lunch with more of the Bollinger, Catherine said, "I'm really tired and sleepy."

"You swam a long way," David said. "We'll make a siesta."

"I want to really sleep," Catherine said.

"Do you feel well, Catherine?" the girl asked.

"Yes. Just deadly sleepy."

"We'll put you to bed," David said. "Do you have a thermometer?" he asked the girl.

"I'm sure I haven't any fever," Catherine said. "I just want to sleep for a long time."

When she was in bed the girl brought in the thermometer and David took Catherine's temperature and her pulse. The temperature was normal and the pulse was one hundred and five.

"The pulse is a little high," he said. "But I don't know your normal pulse."

"I don't either but it's probably too fast."

"I don't think the pulse means much with the temperature normal," David said. "But if you have a fever I'll bring a doctor up from Cannes."

"I don't want a doctor," Catherine said. "I just want to sleep. Can I sleep now?"

"Yes, my beauty. You call if you want me."

They stood and watched her go to sleep and then went out very quietly and David walked along the stones and looked through the window. Catherine was sleeping quietly and her breathing was regular. He brought two chairs up and a table and they sat in the shade near Catherine's window and looked out through the pines to the blue sea. "What do you think?" David asked.

"I don't know. She was happy this morning. Just as you saw her when you finished writing."

"What about now?"

"Maybe just a reaction from yesterday. She's a very natural girl, David, and this is natural."

"Yesterday was like loving someone when someone's died," he said. "It wasn't right." He stood up and walked to the window and looked in. Catherine was sleeping in the same position and breathing lightly. "She's sleeping well," he told the girl. "Wouldn't you like to take a nap?"

"I think so."

"I'm going down to my room where I work," he said. "There's a door to yours that bolts on each side." He walked down along the stones and unlocked the door of his room and then unbolted the door between the two rooms. He stood and waited and then heard the bolt turn on the other side of the door and then the door opened. They sat side by side on the bed and he put his arm around her. "Kiss me," David said.

"I love to kiss you," she said; "I love it so very much. But I can't do the other."

"No?"

"No, I can't."

Then she said, "Isn't there anything I can do for you now? I'm so ashamed about the other but you know how it could make trouble."

"Just lie here by me."

"I'd love that."

"Do what you like."

"I will," she said. "You too please. Do what we can."

Catherine slept all through the afternoon and early evening. David and the girl were sitting at the bar having a drink together and the girl said, "They never did bring the mirror."

"Did you ask old man Aurol about it?"

"Yes. He was pleased."

"I'd better pay him corkage on that Bollinger or something."

"I gave him four bottles and two very good bottles of *fine*. He's taken care of. It was Madame I was afraid of about trouble."

"You were absolutely right."

"I don't want to make trouble, David."

"No," he said. "I don't think you do."

The young waiter had come in with more ice and David made two martinis and gave her one. The waiter put in the garlic olives and then went back to the kitchen.

"I'll go and see how Catherine is," the girl said. "Things will turn out or they won't."

She was gone for about ten minutes and he felt of the girl's drink and decided to drink it before it got warm. He took it in his hand and raised it to his lips and he found as it touched his lips that it gave him pleasure because it was hers. It was clear and undeniable. That's all you need, he thought. That's all you need to make things really perfect. Be in love with both of them. What's happened to you since last May? What are you anymore anyway? But he touched the glass to his lips again and there was the same reaction as before. All right, he said, remember to do the work. The work is what you have left. You better fork up with the work.

The girl came back and when he saw her come in, her face happy, he knew how he felt about her.

"She's getting dressed," the girl said. "She feels fine. Isn't it wonderful?"

"Yes," he said, loving Catherine too as always.

"What happened to my drink?"

"I drank it," he said. "Because it was yours."

"Truly, David?" She blushed and was happy.

"That's as well as I can put it," he said. "Here's a new one."

She tasted it and passed her lips very lightly over the rim and then passed it to him and he did the same and took a long sip. "You're very beautiful," he said. "And I love you."

Chapter Fifteen

HE HEARD THE BUGATTI start and the noise came as a surprise and an intrusion because there was no motor noise in the country where he was living. He was completely detached from everything except the story he was writing and he was living in it as he built it. The difficult parts he had dreaded he now faced one after another and as he did the people, the country, the days and the nights, and the weather were all there as he wrote. He went on working and he felt as tired as if he had spent the night crossing the broken volcanic desert and the sun had caught him and the others with the dry gray lakes still ahead. He could feel the weight of the heavy double-barreled rifle carried over his shoulder, his hand on the muzzle, and he tasted the pebble in his mouth. Across the shimmer of the dry lakes he could see the distant blue of the escarpment. Ahead of him there was no one, and behind was the long line of porters who knew that they had reached this point three hours too late.

It was not him, of course, who had stood there that morning; nor had he even worn the patched corduroy jacket faded almost white now, the armpits rotted through by sweat, that he took off then and handed to his Kamba servant and brother who shared with him the guilt and knowledge of the delay, watching him smell the sour, vinegary smell and shake his head in disgust and then grin as he swung the jacket over his black shoulder holding it by the sleeves as they started off across the dry-baked gray, the gun muzzles in their right hands, the barrels balanced on their shoulders, the heavy stocks pointing back toward the line of porters.

It was not him, but as he wrote it was and when someone read it, finally, it would be whoever read it and what they found when they should reach the escarpment, if they reached it, and he would make them reach its base by noon of that day; then whoever read it would find what there was there and have it always.

All your father found he found for you too, he thought, the good, the wonderful, the bad, the very bad, the really very bad, the truly bad and then the much worse. It was a shame a man with such a talent for disaster and for delight should have gone the way he went, he thought. It always made him happy to remember his father and he knew his father would have liked this story.

It was nearly noon when he came out of the room and walked barefoot on the stones of the patio to the entrance of the hotel. In the big room workmen were putting up a mirror on the wall behind the bar. Monsieur Aurol and the young waiter were with them and he spoke to them and went out in the kitchen where he found Madame.

"Have you any beer, Madame?" he asked her.

"*Mais certainement, Monsieur Bourne,*" she said and brought a cold bottle from the ice chest.

"I'll drink it from the bottle," he said.

"As Monsieur wishes," she said. "The ladies drove to Nice I believe. Monsieur worked well?"

"Very well."

"Monsieur works too hard. It's not good not to take breakfast."

"Is there any of that caviar left in the tin?"

"I'm sure there is."

"I'll take a couple of spoonsful."

"Monsieur is odd," Madame said. "Yesterday you ate it with champagne. Today with beer."

"I'm alone today," David said. "Do you know if my bicyclette is still in the *remise?*"

"It should be," Madame said.

David took a spoonful of the caviar and offered the tin to Madame. "Have some, Madame. It's very good."

"I shouldn't," she said.

"Don't be silly," he told her. "Take some. There's some toast. Take a glass of champagne. There's some in the ice box."

Madame took a spoonful of caviar and put it on a piece of toast left from breakfast and poured herself a glass of rosé.

"It is excellent," she said. "Now we must put it away."

"Do you feel any good effect?" David asked. "I'm going to have one more spoon."

"Ah, Monsieur. You mustn't joke like that."

"Why not?" David said. "My joking partners are away. If those two beautiful women come back tell them I went for a swim will you?"

"Certainly. The little one is a beauty. Not as beautiful as Madame of course."

"I find her not too ugly," David said.

"She's a beauty, Monsieur, and very charming."

"She'll do until something else comes along," David said. "If you think she's pretty."

"Monsieur," she said in deepest reproof.

"What are all the architectural reforms?" David asked.

"The new *miroir* for the bar? It's such a charming gift to the maison."

"Everyone's full of charm," David said. "Charm and sturgeon eggs. Ask the boy to look at my tires while I put something on my feet and find a cap, will you please?"

"Monsieur likes to go barefoot. Me too in summer."

"We'll go barefoot together sometime."

"Monsieur," she said giving it everything.

"Is Aurol jealous?"

"*Sans blague,*" she said. "I'll tell the two beautiful ladies you've gone swimming."

"Keep the caviar away from Aurol," David said. "*À bientôt, chère Madame.*"

"*À tout à l'heure, Monsieur.*"

On the shiny black road that mounted through the pines as he left the hotel he felt the pull in his arms and his shoulders and the rounding thrust of his feet against the pedals as he climbed in the hot sun with the smell of the pines and the light breeze that came from the sea. He bent his back forward and pulled lightly against his hands and felt the cadence that had been ragged as he first mounted begin to smooth out as he passed the hundred-meter stones and then the first red-topped kilometer marker and then the second. At the headland the road dipped to border the sea and he braked and dismounted and put the bicycle over his shoulder and walked down with it along the trail to the beach. He propped it against a pine tree that gave off the resin smell of the hot day and he dropped down to the rocks, stripped and put his espadrilles on his shorts, shirt and cap and he dove from the rocks into the deep clear cold sea. He came up through the varying light and when his head came out he shook it to clear his ears and then swam out to sea. He lay on his back and floated and watched the sky and the first white clouds that were coming with the breeze.

He swam back in to the cove finally and climbed up on the dark red rocks and sat there in the sun looking down into the sea.

He was happy to be alone and to have finished his work for the day. Then the loneliness he always had after work started and he began to think about the girls and to miss them; not to miss the one nor the other at first, but to miss them both. Then he thought of them, not critically, not as any problem of love or fondness, nor of obligation nor of what had happened or would happen, nor of any problem of conduct now or to come, but simply of how he missed them. He was lonely for them both, alone and together, and he wanted them both.

Sitting in the sun on the rock looking down into the sea, he knew it was wrong to want them both but he did. Nothing with either of those two can end well and neither can you now, he told himself. But do not start blaming who you love nor apportioning blame. It will all be apportioned in due time and not by you.

He looked down into the sea and tried to think clearly what the situation was and it did not work out. The worst was what had happened to Catherine. The next worse was that he had begun to care for the other girl. He did not have to examine his conscience to know that he loved Catherine nor that it was wrong to love two women and that no good could ever come of it. He did not yet know how terrible it could be. He only knew that it had started. The three of you are already enmeshed like three gears that turn a wheel, he told himself and also told himself one gear had been stripped or, at least, badly damaged. He dove deep down into the clear cold water where he missed no one and then came up and shook his head and swam out further and then turned to swim back to the beach.

He dressed, still wet from the sea and put his cap in his pocket, then climbed up to the road with his bicycle and mounted, driving the machine up the short hill feeling the lack of training in his thighs as he pressed the balls of his feet on the pedals with the steady climbing thrust that carried him up the black road as though he and the racing bike were some wheeled animal. Then he coasted down, his hands fingering the brakes, taking the curves fast, dropping down the shiny dark road through the pines, to the turnoff at the back court of the hotel where the sea shone summer blue beyond the trees.

The girls were not back yet and he went into the room and took a shower, changed to a fresh shirt and shorts and came out to the bar with its new and handsome mirror. He called the boy and asked him to bring a lemon, a knife and some ice and showed him how to make a Tom Collins. Then he sat on the bar stool and looked into the mirror as he lifted the tall drink. I do not know if I'd have a drink with you or not if I'd met you four months ago, he thought. The boy brought him the *Éclaireur de Nice* and he read it while he waited. He had been disappointed not to find the girls returned and he missed them and began to worry.

When they came in, finally, Catherine was very gay and excited and the girl was contrite and very quiet.

"Hello darling," Catherine said to David. "Oh look at the mirror. They did get it up. It's a very good one too. It's awfully critical though. I'll go in and clean up for lunch. I'm sorry we're late."

"We stopped in town and had a drink," the girl said to David. "I'm sorry to have kept you waiting."

"A drink?" David said.

The girl held up two fingers. She put her face up and kissed him and was gone. David went back to reading the paper.

When Catherine came out she was wearing the dark blue linen shirt that David liked and slacks and she said, "Darling I hope you're not cross. It wasn't really our fault. I saw Jean and I asked him to have a drink with us and he did and was so nice."

"The coiffeur?"

"Jean. Of course. What other Jean would I know in Cannes?

"He was so nice and he asked about you. Can I have a martini, darling? I've only had one."

"Lunch must be ready by now."

"Just one, darling. They only have us for lunch."

David made two martinis taking his time and the girl came in. She was wearing a white sharkskin dress and she looked fresh and cool. "May I have one too, David? It was a very hot day. How was it here?"

"You should have stayed home and looked after him," Catherine said.

"I got along all right," David said. "The sea was very good."

"You use such interesting adjectives," Catherine said. "They make everything so vivid."

"Sorry," David said.

"That's another dandy word," Catherine said. "Explain what dandy means to your new girl. It's an Americanism."

"I think I know it," the girl said. "It's the third word in 'Yankee Doodle Dandy.' Don't please be cross Catherine."

"I'm not cross," Catherine said. "But two days ago when you made passes at me it was simply dandy but today if I felt that way the slightest bit you had to act as though I was an I don't know what."

"I'm sorry, Catherine," the girl said.

"Another sorry sorry," Catherine said. "As though you hadn't taught me what little I know."

"Should we have lunch?" David said. "It's been a hot day Devil, and you're tired."

"I'm tired of everybody," Catherine said. "Please forgive me."

"There's nothing to forgive," the girl said. "I'm sorry I was stuffy. I didn't come here to be that way." She walked over to Catherine and kissed her very gently and lightly. "Now be a good girl," she said. "Should we go to the table?"

"Didn't we have lunch?" Catherine asked.

"No, Devil," David said. "We're going to have lunch now."

At the end of lunch Catherine who had made sense through nearly all of it except for some absentmindedness said, "Please excuse me but I think I ought to sleep."

"Let me come with you and see you get to sleep," the girl said.

"Actually I think I drank too much," Catherine said.

"I'll come in and take a nap too," David said.

"No please David. Come in when I'm asleep if you want," Catherine said.

In about half an hour the girl came out of the room "She's all right," she said. "But we must be careful and good with her and only think about her."

In the room Catherine was awake when David came in and he went over and sat on the bed.

"I'm not a damned invalid," she said. "I just drank too much. I know. I'm sorry I lied to you about it. How could I do that, David?"

"You didn't remember."

"No. I did it on purpose. Will you take me back? I'm over all the bitchiness."

"You never were away."

"If you take me back is all I want. I'll be your really true girl and really truly be. Would you like that?"

He kissed her.

"Really kiss me."

"Oh," she said. "Please be slow."

They swam at the cove where they had gone the first day. David had planned to send the two girls to swim and then to take the old Isotta down to Cannes to have the brakes fixed and the ignition overhauled. But Catherine had asked him to please swim with them and to do the car the next day and she seemed so happy and sound and cheerful again after her nap and Marita had said very seriously, "Will you please come?" So he had driven them to the turnout for the cove and shown them both on the way how dangerously the brakes were working.

"You'd kill yourself with this car," he told Marita. "It's a crime to drive it the way it is."

"Had I ought to get a new one?" she asked.

"Christ no. Just let me fix the brakes to start with."

"We need a larger car with room for all of us," Catherine said.

"This is a fine car," David said. "It just needs a hell of a lot of work done on it. But it's too much car for you."

"You see if they can fix it properly," the girl said. "If they can't we'll get the type of car you want."

Then they were tanning on the beach and David said lazily, "Come in and swim."

"Pour some water on my head," Catherine said. "I brought a sand bucket in the rucksack."

"Oh that feels wonderful," she said. "Could I have one more? Pour it on my face too."

She lay on the hard beach on her white robe in the sun and David and the girl swam out to sea and around the rocks at the mouth of the cove. The girl was swimming ahead and David overhauled her. He reached out and grabbed a foot and then held her close in his arms and kissed her as they treaded water. She felt slippery and strange in the water and they seemed the same height as they treaded water with their bodies close together and kissed. Then her head went under and he leaned back and she came up laughing and shaking her head that was sleek as a seal, and she brought her lips against his again and they kissed until they both went under. They lay side by side and floated and touched and then kissed hard and happily and went under again.

"I don't worry about anything now," she said, when they came up again. "You mustn't either."

"I won't," he said and they swam in.

"You better go in, Devil," he said to Catherine. "Your head will get too hot."

"All right. Let's go in," she said. "Let Heiress darken now. Let me put some oil on her."

"Not too much," the girl said. "May I have a pail of water on my head too?"

"Your head's as wet as it can get," Catherine said.

"I just wanted to feel it," the girl said.

"Wade out, David, and get a good cold one," Catherine said. And after he had poured the clear cool sea water on Marita's head they left her lying with her face on her arms and swam out to sea. They floated easily like sea animals and Catherine said, "Wouldn't it be wonderful if I wasn't crazy?"

"You're not crazy."

"Not this afternoon," she said. "Anyway not so far. Can we swim further?"

"We're pretty well out, Devil."

"All right. Let's swim back in. But the deep water's beautiful out here."

"Do you want to swim down once before we go in?"

"Just once," she said. "In this very deep part."

"We'll swim down until we just can make it up."

Chapter Sixteen

HE WOKE when it was barely just light enough to see the pine trunks and he left the bed, careful not to wake Catherine, found his shorts and went, the soles of his feet wet from the dew on the stones, along the length of the hotel to the door of his work room. As he opened the door he felt, again, the touch of the air from the sea that promised how the day would be.

When he sat down the sun was not yet up and he felt that he had made up some of the time that was lost in the story. But as he reread his careful legible hand and the words took him away and into the other country, he lost that advantage and was faced with the same problem and when the sun rose out of the sea it had, for him, risen long before and he was well into the crossing of the gray, dried, bitter lakes his boots now white with crusted alkalis. He felt the weight of the sun on his head and his neck and his back. His shirt was wet and he felt the sweat go down his back and between his thighs. When he stood straight up and rested, breathing slowly, and his shirt hung away from his shoulders, he could feel it dry in the sun and see the white patches that the salts of his body made in the drying. He could feel and see himself standing there and knew there was nothing to do except go on.

At half past ten he had crossed the lakes and was well beyond them. By then he had reached the river and the great grove of fig trees where they would make their camp. The bark of the trunks was green and yellow and the branches were heavy. Baboons had been eating the wild figs and there were baboon droppings and broken figs on the ground. The smell was foul.

But the half past ten was on the watch on his wrist as he looked at it in the room where he sat at a table feeling the breeze from the sea now and the real time was evening and he was sitting against the yellow gray base of a tree with a glass of whiskey and water in his hand and the rolled figs swept away watching the porters butchering out the Kongoni he had shot in the first grassy swale they passed before they came to the river.

I'll leave them with meat, he thought and so it is a happy camp tonight no matter what comes after. So he put his pencils and the notebooks away and locked the suitcase and went out the door and walked on the stones, dry and warm now, to the hotel patio.

The girl was sitting at one of the tables reading a book. She wore a striped fisherman's shirt and tennis skirt and espadrilles and when she saw him she looked up and David thought she was going to blush but she seemed to check it and said, "Good morning, David. Did you work well?"

"Yes, beauty," he said.

She stood up then and kissed him good morning and said, "I'm very happy then. Catherine went in to Cannes. She said to tell you I was to take you swimming."

"Didn't she want you to go in town with her?"

"No. She wanted me to stay. She said you got up terribly early to work and maybe you'd be lonely when you finished. Can I order some breakfast? You shouldn't always not eat breakfast."

The girl went into the kitchen and she came out with *oeufs au plat avec jambon* and English mustard and Sovora.

"Was it difficult today?" she asked him.

"No," he said. "It's always difficult but it's easy too. It went very well."

"I wish I could help."

"Nobody can help," he said.

"But I can help in other things can't I?"

He started to say there are no other things but he did not say it and instead he said, "You have and you do."

He wiped the last of the egg and mustard up from the shallow dish with a small piece of bread and then drank some tea. "How did you sleep?" he asked.

"Very well," the girl said. "I hope that's not disloyal."

"No. That's intelligent."

"Can we stop being so polite?" the girl asked. "Everything was so simple and fine until now."

"Yes, let's stop. Let's stop even the 'I can't David' nonsense," he said.

"All right," she said and stood up. "If you want to go swimming I'll be in my room."

He stood up. "Please don't go," he said. "I've stopped being a shit."

"Don't stop for me," she said. "Oh David how could we ever get in a thing like this? Poor David. What women do to you." She was stroking his head and smiling at him. "I'll get the swimming things if you want to swim."

"Good," he said. "I'll go get my espadrilles."

·   ·   ·

They lay on the sand where David had spread the beach robes and the towels in the shade of a red rock and the girl said, "You go in and swim and then I will."

He lifted very slowly and gently up out and away from her and then waded out from the beach and dove under where the water was cold and swam deep. When he came up he swam out against the chop of the breeze and then swam in to where the girl was waiting for him standing up to her waist in the water her black head sleek and wet, her light brown body dripping. He held her tight and the waves washed against them.

They kissed and she said, "Everything of ours washed into the ocean."

"We have to get back."

"Let's go under once together holding tight."

Back at the hotel Catherine had not arrived and after they had taken showers and changed David and Marita sat at the bar with two martinis. They looked at each other in the mirror. They watched each other very carefully and then David passed his finger under his nose while he looked at her and she blushed.

"I want to have more things like that," she said. "Things that only we have so I won't be jealous."

"I wouldn't put out too many anchors," he said. "You might foul the cables."

"No. I'll find things to do that will hold you."

"That's a good practical Heiress," he said.

"I wish I could change that name. Don't you?"

"Names go to the bone," he said.

"Then let's really change mine," she said. "Would you mind terribly?"

"No. . . . *Haya.*"

"Say it again please."

"Haya."

"Is it good?"

"Very good. It's a small name between us. For nobody else ever."

"What does Haya mean?"

"The one who blushes. The modest one."

He held her close and tight and she settled against him and her head was on his shoulder.

"Kiss me just once," she said.

Catherine came into the big room dishevelled, excited and full of accomplishment and gaiety.

"You *did* take him swimming," she said. "You both do look handsome enough, though still wet from the shower. Let me look at you."

"Let me look at *you*," the girl said. "What did you do to your hair?"

"It's *cendre*," Catherine said. "Do you like it? It's a rinse that Jean's experimenting with."

"It's beautiful," the girl said.

Catherine's hair was strange and exalting against her dark face. She picked up Marita's drink and sipping it watched herself in the mirror and said, "Did you have fun swimming?"

"We both had a good swim," the girl said. "But not as long as yesterday."

"This is such a good drink, David," Catherine said. "What makes your martinis better than anyone else's?"

"Gin," David said.

"Will you make me one please?"

"You don't want one now, Devil. We're going to have lunch."

"Yes I do," she said. "I'm going to sleep after lunch. You

didn't have to go through all the bleaching and re-bleaching and all of it. It's exhausting."

"What color is your hair really now?" David asked.

"It's almost like white," she said. "You'd like it. But I want to keep this so we see how it lasts."

"How white is it?" David asked.

"About like the soap suds," she said. "Do you remember?"

That evening Catherine was completely different from the way she had been at mid-day. She was sitting at the bar when they drove up from swimming. The girl had stopped off at her room and when David came into the big main room he said, "What have you done to yourself now, Devil?"

"I shampooed all that nonsense out," she said. "It made gray stains on the pillow."

She looked very striking, her hair a very light almost toneless silver that made her face darker than it had ever looked.

"You're too damned beautiful," he said. "But I wish they'd never touched your hair."

"It's too late for that now. Can I tell you something else?"

"Sure."

"Tomorrow I'm not going to have drinks and I'm going to study Spanish and read again and stop thinking only about myself."

"My God," David said. "You had a big day. Here, let me get a drink and go in and change."

"I'll be here," Catherine said. "Put on your dark blue shirt will you? The one I got you like the one of mine?"

David took his time in the shower and changing and when he came back the two girls were together at the bar and he wished he could have a painting of them.

"I told Heiress everything about my new leaf," Catherine said. "The one I just turned over and how I want you to love her too and you can marry her too if she'll have you."

"We could in Africa if I was registered Mohammedan. You're allowed three wives."

"I think it would be much nicer if we were all married," Catherine said. "Then no one could criticize us. Will you really marry him, Heiress?"

"Yes," the girl said.

"I'm so pleased," Catherine said. "Everything I worried about is so simple now."

"Would you really?" David asked the dark girl.

"Yes," she said. "Ask me."

David looked at her. She was very serious and excited. He thought of her face with her eyes closed against the sun and her black head against the whiteness of the towel robe on the yellow sand as it had been when they had made love at last. "I'll ask you," he said. "But not in any damned bar."

"This isn't any damned bar," Catherine said. "This is our own special bar and we bought the mirror. I wish we could marry you tonight."

"Don't talk balls," David said.

"I'm not," Catherine said. "I really mean it. Truly."

"Do you want a drink?" David asked.

"No," Catherine said. "I want to get it said right first. Look at me and see." The girl was looking down and David looked at Catherine. "I thought it all out this afternoon," she said. "I really did. Didn't I tell you, Marita?"

"She did," the girl said.

David saw that she was serious about this and that they had reached some understanding that he did not know about.

"I'm still your wife," Catherine said. "We'll start with that. I want Marita to be your wife too to help me out and then she inherits from me."

"Why does she have to inherit?"

"People make their wills," she said. "And this is more important than a will."

"What about you?" David asked the girl.

"I want to do it if you want me to."

"Good," he said. "Do you mind if I have a drink?"

"You have one please," Catherine said. "You see I'm not going to have you ruined if I'm crazy and I won't be able to decide. I'm not going to be shut up either. I decided that too. She loves you and you love her a little. I can tell. You'd never find anybody else like her and I don't want you to go to some damn bitch or be lonely."

"Come on and cheer up," David said. "You're healthy as a goat."

"Well, we're going to do it," Catherine said. "We'll work out everything."

Chapter Seventeen

THE SUN WAS BRIGHT now in the room and it was a new day. You better get to work, he told himself. You can't change any of it back. Only one person can change it back and she can't know how she will wake nor if she'll be there when she wakes. It doesn't matter how you feel. You better get to work. You have to make sense there. You don't make any in this other. Nothing will help you. Nor would have ever since it started.

When he finally got back into the story the sun was well up and he had forgotten the two girls. It had been necessary to think what his father would have thought sitting that evening with his back against the green-yellow trunk of the fig tree with the enameled cup of whiskey and water in his hand. His father had dealt so lightly with evil, giving it no chance ever and denying its importance so that it had no status and no shape nor dignity. He treated evil like an old entrusted friend, David thought, and evil, when she poxed him, never knew she'd scored. His father was not vulnerable he knew and, unlike most people he had known, only death could kill him. Finally, he knew what his father had thought and knowing it, he did not put it in the story. He only wrote what his father did and how he felt and in all this he became his father and what his father said to Molo was what he said. He slept well on the ground under the tree and he waked and heard the leopard cough. Later he did not hear the leopard in the camp but he knew he was there and he went back to sleep. The leopard was after meat and there was plenty of meat so there was no problem. In the morning before daylight sitting by the ashes of the fire with his tea in the chipped enameled cup he asked Molo if the leopard had taken meat and Molo said, "Ndiyo" and he said, "There's plenty where we're going. Get them moving so we can start the climb."

They were moving for the second day through the high wooded and park-like country above the escarpment when he stopped finally and he was happy with the country and the day and the distance they had made. He had his father's ability to forget now and not dread anything that was coming. There was another day and another night ahead in that new high country when he stopped and he had lived two days and a night today.

Now that he left that country his father was with him still as he locked the door and walked back to the big room and the bar.

He told the boy he did not want breakfast and to bring him a whiskey and Perrier and the morning paper. It was past noon and he had intended to drive the old Isotta into Cannes and see that the repairs were made but he knew the garages were closed now and it was too late. Instead he stood at the bar because that's where he would have found his father at that hour and, having just come down from the high country, he missed him. The sky outside was very much the sky that he had left. It was high blue and the clouds white cumulus and he welcomed his father's presence at the bar until he glanced in the mirror and saw he was alone. He had intended to ask his father about two things. His father, who ran his life more disastrously than any man that he had ever known, gave marvelous advice. He distilled it out of the bitter mash of all his previous mistakes with the freshening addition of the new mistakes he was about to make and he gave it with an accuracy and precision that carried the authority of a man who had heard all the more grisly provisions of his sentence and gave it no more importance than he had given to the fine print on a transatlantic steamship ticket.

He was sorry that his father had not stayed but he could hear the advice clearly enough and he smiled. His father would have given it more exactly but he, David, had stopped writing because he was tired and, tired, he could not do justice to his father's style. No one could, really, and sometimes his father could not either. He knew now, more than ever, why he had always put off writing this story and he knew he must not think about it now that he had left it or he would damage his ability to write it.

You must not worry about it before you start nor when you stop he told himself. You're lucky to have it and don't start fumbling with it now. If you cannot respect the way you handle your life then certainly respect your trade. You know about your trade at least. But it was a rather awful story really. By God it was.

He sipped the whiskey and Perrier again and looked out the door at the late summer day. He was cooling out as he always did and the giant killer made things better. He wondered where the girls were. They were late again and he hoped that this time it would be nothing bad. He was not a tragic character, having his father and being a writer barred him from that, and as he finished the whiskey and Perrier he felt even less of one. He had never known a morning when he had not waked happily until the enormity of the day had touched him and he had accepted this day now as he had accepted all the others for himself. He had lost the capacity of personal suffering, or he thought he had, and only could be hurt truly by what happened to others. He believed this, wrongly of course since he did not know then how one's capacities can change, nor how the other could change, and it was a comfortable belief. He thought of the two girls and wished that they would turn up. It was getting too late to swim before lunch but he wanted to see them. He thought about them both. Then he went into his and Catherine's room and took a shower and shaved. He was shaving when he heard the car come up and he felt the sudden empty feeling in his gut. Then he heard their voices and heard them laughing and he found a fresh pair of shorts and a shirt and pulled them on and went out to see how things would be.

The three of them had quiet drinks and then a lunch that was good but light and they drank Tavel and when they were eating cheese and fruit Catherine said, "Should I tell him?"

"If you want," the girl said. She picked up her wine and drank part of it down.

"I forgot how to say it," Catherine said. "We waited too long."

"Can't you remember it?" the girl said.

"No, I've forgotten it and it was wonderful. We had it all worked out and it was really wonderful."

David poured himself another glass of Tavel.

"Do you want to try for just the factual content?" he asked.

"I know the factual content," Catherine said. "It's that yesterday you made siesta with me and then you went to Marita's room but today you can just go there. But I've spoiled it now and what I wish is we could all just make siesta together."

"Not siesta," David heard himself say.

"I suppose not," Catherine said. "Well I'm sorry I said it all wrong and I couldn't help saying what I wished."

In the room he said to Catherine, "To hell with her."

"No, David. She wanted to do what I asked her. Maybe she can tell you."

"Fuck her."

"Well you have," she said. "That's not the point. Go and talk with her David. And if you want to fuck her then fuck her good for me."

"Don't talk rough."

"You used it. I just knocked it back. Like tennis."

"All right," David said. "What's she supposed to say to me?"

"My speech," Catherine said. "The one I forgot. Don't look so serious or I won't let you go. You're awfully appealing when you're serious. You'd better go before she forgets the speech."

"The hell with you too."

"That's good. Now you're reacting better. I like you when you are more careless. Kiss me goodbye. I mean good afternoon. You really better go or she really will forget the speech. Don't you see how reasonable and good I am?"

"You're not reasonable and good."

"You like me though."

"Sure."

"Do you want me to tell you a secret?"

"A new one?"

"An old one."

"All right."

"You aren't very hard to corrupt and you're an awful lot of fun to corrupt."

"You ought to know."

"It was just a joke secret. There isn't any corruption. We just have fun. Go on in and have her make my speech before she forgets it too. Go on and be a good boy David."

In the room at the far end of the hotel David lay on the bed and said, "What's it all about really?"

"It's just what she said last night," the girl said. "She really means it. You don't know how much she means it."

"Did you tell her we'd made love?"

"No."

"She knew it."

"Does it matter?"

"It didn't seem to."

"Take a glass of wine, David, and be comfortable. I'm not in-different," she said. "I hope you know that."

"I'm not either," he said.

Then their lips were together and he felt her body against his and her breasts against his chest and her lips tight against his and then open, her head moving from side to side and her breathing and the feel of his belt buckle against his belly and in his hands.

They lay on the beach and David watched the sky and the movement of the clouds and did not think at all. Thinking did no good and when he lay down he had thought that if he did not think then everything that was wrong might go away. The girls were talking but he did not listen to them. He lay and watched the September sky and when the girls had fallen silent he started to think and without looking at the girl he asked, "What are you thinking?"

"Nothing," she said.

"Ask me," Catherine said.

"I can guess what you're thinking."

"No you can't. I was thinking about the Prado."

"Have you been there?" David asked the girl.

"Not yet," she said.

"We'll go," Catherine said. "When can we go, David?"

"Anytime," David said. "I want to finish this story first."

"Will you work hard on the story?"

"That's what I'm doing. I can't work any harder."

"I didn't mean to hurry it."

"I won't," he said. "If you're getting bored here you two go on ahead and I'll find you there."

"I don't want to do that," Marita said.

"Don't be silly," Catherine said. "He's just being noble."

"No. You can go."

"It wouldn't be any fun without you," Catherine said. "You know that. We two in Spain wouldn't be fun."

"He's working, Catherine," Marita said.

"He could work in Spain," Catherine said. "Plenty of Spanish writers must have worked in Spain. I'll bet I could write well in Spain if I was a writer."

"I can write in Spain," David said. "When do you want to go?"

"Damn you, Catherine," Marita said. "He's in the middle of a story."

"He's been writing for over six weeks," Catherine said. "Why can't we go to Madrid?"

"I said we could," David said.

"Don't you dare do that," the girl said to Catherine. "Don't you dare to try to do that. Haven't you any conscience at all?"

"You're a fine one to talk about conscience," Catherine said.

"I have a conscience about some things."

"That's fine. I'm happy to know it. Now will you try to be polite and not interfere when someone is trying to work out what's best for everyone?"

"I'm going to swim," David said.

The girl got up and followed him and outside the cove while they treaded water she said, "She's crazy."

"So don't blame her."

"But what are you going to do?"

"Finish the story and start another."

"So what do you and I do?"

"What we can."

Chapter Eighteen

HE FINISHED THE STORY in four days. He had in it all the pressure that had built while he was writing it and the modest part of him was afraid that it could not possibly be as good as he believed it to be. The cold, hard part knew it was better.

"How was it today?" the girl asked him.

"I finished."

"Can I read it?"

"If you want to."

"You wouldn't mind truly?"

"It's in those two cahiers in the top of the suitcase." He handed her the key and then sat at the bar and drank a whiskey and Perrier and read the morning paper. She came back and sat on a stool a little way down from him and read the story.

When she finished it she started to read it over again and he made himself a second whiskey and soda and watched her read. When she finished it the second time he said, "Do you like it?"

"It's not a thing you like or not like," she said. "It's your father isn't it?"

"Sure."

"Was this when you stopped loving him?"

"No. I always loved him. This was when I got to know him."

"It's a terrible story and it's wonderful."

"I'm glad you like it," he said.

"I'll put it back now," she said. "I like going in the room when the door is locked."

"We have that," David said.

When they came back from the beach they found Catherine in the garden.

"So you got back," she said.

"Yes," David said. "We had a good swim. I wish you'd been there."

"Well, I wasn't," she said. "If it's of any interest to you."

"Where did you go?" David asked.

"I was in Cannes on my own business," she said. "You're both late for lunch."

"I'm sorry," David said. "Do you want to have anything before lunch?"

"Please excuse me, Catherine," Marita said. "I'll be back in a moment."

"You're still drinking before lunch?" Catherine asked David.

"Yes," he said. "I don't think it matters if you're getting a lot of exercise."

"There was an empty whiskey glass on the bar when I came in."

"Yes," said David. "I had two whiskeys actually."

"Actually," she mimicked him. "You're very British today."

"Really?" he said. "I didn't feel very British. I felt sort of half-assed Tahitian."

"It's just your way of speaking that irritates me," she said. "Your choice of words."

"I see," he said. "Did you want a shot before they bring the chow?"

"You don't have to be a clown."

"The best clowns don't talk," he said.

"Nobody accused you of being the best of clowns," she said. "Yes. I'd like a drink if it isn't too much work for you to make it."

He made three martinis, measuring them each out separately and pouring them into the pitcher where there was a big chunk of ice and then stirring.

"Who is the third drink for?"

"Marita."

"Your paramour?"

"My what?"

"Your paramour."

"You really said it," David told her. "I'd never heard that word pronounced and I had absolutely no hope of ever hearing it in this life. You're really wonderful."

"It's a perfectly common word."

"It is at that," David said. "But to have the sheer, naked courage to use it in conversation. Devil, be good now. Couldn't you say 'your dusky paramour'?"

Catherine looked away as she raised her glass.

"And I used to find this type of banter amusing," she said.

"Do you want to try to be decent?" David asked. "Both of us decent?"

"No," she said. "Here comes your whatever you call her looking sweet and innocent as ever. I must say I'm glad I had her before you did. *Dear* Marita—tell me, did David work before he started drinking today?"

"Did you David?" Marita asked.

"I finished a story," David said.

"And I suppose Marita's already read it?"

"Yes, I did."

"You know, I've never read a story of David's. I never interfere. I've only tried to make it economically possible for him to do the best work of which he is capable."

David took a sip of his drink and looked at her. She was the same wonderful dark and beautiful girl as ever and the ivory white hair was like a scar across her forehead. Only her eyes had changed and her lips that were saying things they were incapable of saying.

"I thought it was a very good story," Marita said. "It was strange and how do you say *pastorale*. Then it became terrible in a way I could not explain. I thought it was *magnifique*."

"Well—," Catherine said. "We all speak French you know. You might have made the whole emotional outburst in French."

"I was deeply moved by the story," Marita said.

"Because David wrote it or because it really is first rate?"

"Both," the girl said.

"Well," Catherine said, "is there any reason then why I can't read this extraordinary story? I did put up the money for it."

"You did what?" David asked.

"Perhaps not exactly. You did have fifteen hundred dollars when you married me and that book about all the mad fliers has sold, hasn't it? You never tell me how much. But I did put up a substantial sum and you must admit you've lived more comfortably than you did before you married me."

The girl did not say anything and David watched the waiter setting the table on the terrace. He looked at his watch. It was about twenty minutes before the time they usually had lunch. "I'd like to go in and clean up if I may," he said.

"Don't be so bloody false polite," Catherine said. "Why can't I read the story?"

"It's just written in pencil. It hasn't even been copied. You wouldn't want to read it that way."

"Marita read it that way."

"Read it after lunch then."

"I want to read it now, David."

"I really wouldn't read it before lunch."

"Is it disgusting?"

"It's a story about Africa back before the 1914 War. In the time of the Maji-Maji War. The native rebellion of 1905 in Tanganyika."

"I didn't know you wrote historical novels."

"I wish you'd leave it alone," David said. "It's a story that happens in Africa when I was about eight years old."

"I want to read it."

David had gone to the far end of the bar and was shaking dice out of a leather cup. The girl sat on a stool next to Catherine. He watched her watching Catherine as she read.

"It starts very well," she said. "Though your handwriting is atrocious. The country is superb. The passage. What Marita miscalled the *pastorale* part."

She put down the first notebook and the girl picked it up and held it on her lap, her eyes still watching Catherine.

Catherine read on and said nothing now. She was halfway through the second part. Then she tore the cahier in two and threw it on the floor.

"It's horrible," she said. "It's bestial. So that was what your father was like."

"No," said David. "But that was one way he was. You didn't finish it."

"Nothing would make me finish it."

"I didn't want you to read it at all."

"No. You both conspired to make me read it."

"May I have the key, David, to lock it up?" the girl asked. She had retrieved the torn halves of the notebook from the floor. It was just ripped apart. It was not torn across. David gave her his key.

"It's even more horrible written in that child's notebook," Catherine said. "You're a monster."

"It was a very odd rebellion," David said.

"You're a very odd person to write about it," she said.

"I asked you not to read the story."

She was crying now. "I hate you," she said.

They were in their room in bed and it was late.

"She'll go away and you'll have me shut up or put away," Catherine said.

"No. That isn't true."

"But you suggested we go to Switzerland."

"If you were worried we could see a good doctor. The same way we'd go to the dentist."

"No. They'd shut me up. I know. Everything that's innocent to us is crazy to them. I know about those places."

"It's an easy drive and beautiful. We'd go by Aix and St. Remy and up the Rhone from Lyon to Geneva. We'd see him and get some good advice and make a fun trip out of it."

"I won't go."

"A very good intelligent doctor that—"

"I won't go. Didn't you hear me? I won't go. I won't go. Do you want me to scream?"

"All right. Don't think about it now. Just try to sleep."

"If I don't have to go."

"We don't have to."

"I'll sleep then. Are you going to work in the morning?"

"Yes. I might as well."

"You'll work well," she said. "I know you will. Good night David. You sleep well too."

He did not sleep for a long time. When he did he had dreams of Africa. They were good dreams until the one that woke him. He got up then and went direct from that dream to work. He was well into the new story before the sun came up out of the sea and he did not look up from where he was to see how red the sun was. In the story he was waiting for the moon to rise and he felt his dog's hair rise under his hand as he stroked him to be quiet and they both watched and listened as the moon came up and gave them shadows. His arm was around the dog's neck now and he could feel him shivering. All of the night sounds had stopped. They did not hear the elephant and David did not see him until the dog turned his head and seemed to settle into David. Then the elephant's shadow covered them and he moved past making no noise at all and they smelled him in the light wind that came down from the mountain. He smelled strong but old and sour and when he was past David saw that the left tusk was so long it seemed to reach the ground. They waited but no other elephants came by and then David and the dog started off running in the moonlight. The dog kept close behind him and when David stopped the dog pressed his muzzle into the back of his knee. David had to see the bull again and they came up on him at the edge of the forest. He was travelling toward the mountain and slowly now moving into the steady night breeze. David came close enough to see him cut off the moon again and to smell the sour oldness but he could not see the right tusk. He was afraid to work closer with the dog and he took him back with the wind and pushed him down against the base of a tree and tried to make him understand. He thought the dog would stay and he did but when David moved up toward the bulk of the elephant again he felt the wet muzzle against the hollow of his knee.

The two of them followed the elephant until he came to an opening in the trees. He stood there moving his huge ears. His bulk was in the shadow but the moon would be on his head. David reached behind him and closed the dog's jaws gently with his hand and then moved softly and unbreathing to his right along the edge of the night breeze feeling it on his cheek, edging with it, never letting it get between him and the bulk until he could see the elephant's head and the great ears slowly moving. The right tusk was as thick as his own thigh and it curved down almost to the ground.

He and the dog moved back, the wind on his neck now, and they backtracked out of the forest and into the open park country. The dog was ahead of him now and he stopped where David had left the two hunting spears by the trail when they had followed the elephant. He swung them over his shoulder in their thong and leather cup harness and, with his best spear that he had kept with him all the time in his hand, they started on the trail for the shamba. The moon was high now and he wondered why there was no drumming from the shamba. Something was strange if his father was there and there was no drumming.

Chapter Nineteen

THEY WERE LYING on the firm sand of the smallest of the three coves, the one they always went to when they were alone, and the girl said, "She won't go to Switzerland."

"She shouldn't go to Madrid either. Spain is a bad place to crack up."

"I feel as though we'd been married all our lives and never had anything but problems." She pushed his hair back from his forehead and kissed him. "Do you want to swim now?"

"Yes. Let's dive from the high rock. The really high one."

"You do," she said. "I'll swim out and you dive over my head."

"All right. But hold still when I dive."

"See how close you can come."

Looking up, she watched him poised on the high rock, arced brown against the blue sky. Then he came toward her and the water rose in a spout from a hole in the water behind her shoulder. He turned under water and came up in front of her and shook his head. "I cut it too fine," he said.

They swam out to the point and back and then wiped each other dry and dressed on the beach.

"You really liked me diving that close?"

"I loved it."

He kissed her and she felt cool and fresh from the swimming and she still tasted of the sea.

Catherine came in while they were still sitting at the bar. She was tired and quiet and polite.

At the table she said, "I went to Nice and then drove the little Corniche and I stopped up above Villefranche and watched a battle cruiser come in and then it was late."

"You weren't very late," Marita said.

"But it was very strange," Catherine said. "All the colors were too bright. Even the grays were bright. The olive trees were glittery."

"That's the noon light," David said.

"No. I don't think so," she said. "It wasn't very nice and it was lovely when I stopped to watch the ship. She didn't look big to have such a big name."

"Please eat some of the steak," David said. "You've eaten hardly anything."

"I'm sorry," she said. "It's good. I like tournedos."

"Would you like something instead of the meat?"

"No. I'll eat the salad. Do you think we could have a bottle of the Perrier-Jouët?"

"Of course."

"It was always such a nice wine," she said. "And we were always so happy with it."

Afterward in their room Catherine said, "Don't worry, David, please. It's just speeded up so much lately."

"How?" he asked. He was stroking her forehead.

"I don't know. All of a sudden I was old this morning and it wasn't even the right time of year. Then the colors started to be false. I worried and wanted to get you taken care of."

"You take wonderful care of everybody."

"I'm going to but I was so tired and there wasn't any time and I knew it would be so humiliating if the money ran out and you had to borrow and I hadn't fixed up anything nor signed anything and just been sloppy the way I've been. Then I worried about your dog."

"My dog?"

"Yes your dog in Africa in the story. I went in the room to see if you needed anything and I read the story. While you and Marita were talking in the other room. I didn't listen. You left your keys in the shorts you changed from."

"It's about half through," he told her.

"It's wonderful," she said. "But it frightens me. The elephant was so strange and your father too. I never liked him but I like the dog better than anyone except you David, and I'm so worried about him."

"He was a wonderful dog. You don't have to worry about him."

"Can I read about what happened to him today in the story?"

"Sure, if you want to. But he's at the shamba now and you don't need to worry about him."

"If he's all right I won't read it until you get back to him. Kibo. He had a lovely name."

"It's the name of a mountain. The other part is Mawenzi."

"You and Kibo. I love you so much. You were so much alike."

"You're feeling better, Devil."

"Probably," Catherine said. "I hope so. But it won't last. Driving this morning I was so very happy and then suddenly I was old, so old I didn't care anymore."

"You're not old."

"Yes I am. I'm older than my mother's old clothes and I won't outlive your dog. Not even in a story."

Chapter Twenty

DAVID HAD FINISHED writing and he was empty and hollow-feeling from having driven himself long past the point where he should have stopped. He did not think it mattered that day because it was the exhaustion part of the story and so he had felt the tiredness as soon as they had picked up the trail again. For a long time he had been fresher and in better shape than the two men and impatient with their slow trailing and the regular halts his father made each hour on the hour. He could have moved ahead much faster than Juma and his father but when he started to tire they were the same as ever and at noon they took only the usual five minute rest and he had seen that Juma was increasing the pace a little. Perhaps he wasn't. Perhaps it had only seemed faster but the dung was fresher now although it was not warm yet to the touch. Juma gave him the rifle to carry after they came on the last pile of dung but after an hour he looked at him and took it back. They had been climbing steadily across a slope of the mountain but now the trail went down and from a gap in the forest he saw the broken country ahead.

"Here's where the tough part starts, Davey," his father said.

It was then he knew that he should have been sent back to the shamba once he had put them on the trail. Juma had known it for a long time. His father knew it now and there was nothing to be done. It was another of his mistakes and there was nothing to do now except gamble. David looked down at the big flattened circle of the print of the elephant foot and saw where the bracken had been pressed down and where a broken stem of a flowering weed was drying beyond the break. Juma picked it up and looked at the sun. Juma handed the broken weed to David's father and his father rolled it in his fingers. David noticed the white flowers that were drooped and drying. But they still had not dried in the sun nor shed their petals.

"It's going to be a bitch," his father said. "Let's get going."

Late in the afternoon they were still tracking through the broken country. He had been sleepy now for a long time and as he watched the two men he knew that sleepiness was his real enemy and he followed their pace and tried to move through and out of the sleep that deadened him. The two men relieved each other tracking on the hour and the one who was in second place looked back at him at regular intervals to check if he was with them. When they made a dry camp at dark in the forest again he went to sleep as soon as he sat down and woke with Juma holding his moccasins and feeling his bare feet for blisters. His father had spread his coat over him and was sitting by him with a piece of cold cooked meat and two biscuits. He offered him a water bottle with cold tea.

"He'll have to feed, Davey," his father said. "Your feet are in good shape. They're as sound as Juma's. Eat this slowly and drink some tea and go to sleep again. We haven't any problem."

"I'm sorry I was so sleepy."

"You and Kibo hunted and travelled all last night. Why shouldn't you be sleepy? You can have a little more meat if you want it."

"I'm not hungry."

"Good. We're good for three days. We'll hit water again to-morrow. Plenty of creeks come off the mountain."

"Where's he going?"

"Juma thinks he knows."

"Isn't it bad?"

"Not too bad, Davey."

"I'm going back to sleep," David had said. "I don't need your coat."

"Juma and I are all right," his father said. "I always sleep warm you know."

David was asleep even before his father said good night. Then he woke once with the moonlight on his face and he thought of the elephant with his great ears moving as he stood in the forest, his head hung down with the weight of the tusks. David thought then in the night that the hollow way he felt as he remembered him was from waking hungry. But it was not and he found that out in the next three days.

In the story he had tried to make the elephant come alive again as he and Kibo had seen him in the night when the moon had risen. Maybe I can, David thought, maybe I can. But as he locked up the day's work and went out of the room and shut the door he told himself, No, you can't do it. The elephant was old and if it had not been your father it would have been someone else. There is nothing you can do except try to write it the way that it was. So you must write each day better than you possibly can and use the sorrow that you have now to make you know how the early sorrow came. And you must always remember the things you believed because if you know them they will be there in the writing and you won't betray them. The writing is the only progress you make.

He went behind the bar and found the bottle of Haig and a cold half bottle of Perrier and made himself a drink and took it out in the big kitchen to find Madame. He told her he was going into Cannes and would not be back for lunch. She scolded him about drinking whiskey on an empty stomach and he asked her what she had cold that he could put in the empty stomach with the whiskey. She brought out some cold chicken and sliced it and put it on a plate and made an endive salad and he went into the bar and made another drink and came back to sit down at the kitchen table.

"Don't drink that now before you eat, Monsieur," Madame said.

"It's good for me," he told her. "We drank it at the mess like wine in the war."

"It's a wonder you weren't all drunkards."

"Like the French," he said and they argued French working class drinking habits, on which they both agreed, and she teased him that his women had left him. He said that he was tired of them both and wasn't she ready to take their place now? No, she said, he would have to show more evidence he was a man before he roused a woman of the Midi. He said he was going into Cannes where he could get a proper meal and would come back like a lion and let the women of the south take care. They kissed affectionately with the kiss of the favoured client and the brave *femme* and then David went in to take a shower, to shave and to change.

The shower made him feel good and he was cheered up from talking to Madame. I wonder what she would say if she knew what it was all about, he thought. Things had changed since the war and both Monsieur and Madame had a sense of style and they wished to move with the change. We three clients are all *de gens très bien.* So long as it pays and isn't violent there is nothing wrong with it. The Russians are gone, the British are beginning to be poor, the Germans are ruined, and now there is this disregard of the established rules which can very well be the salvation of the whole coast. We are pioneers in opening up the summer season which is still regarded as madness. He looked at his face in the mirror with one side shaved. Still, he said to himself, you don't need to be such a pioneer as not to shave the other side. And then he noted with careful critical distaste the almost silvery whiteness of his hair.

He heard the Bugatti come up the long slope and turn onto the gravel and stop.

Catherine came into the room. She had a scarf over her head and sunglasses on and she took them off and kissed David. He held her close and said, "How are you?"

"Not so good," she said. "It was too hot." She smiled at him and put her forehead on his shoulder. "I'm glad I'm home."

He went out and made a Tom Collins and brought it in to Catherine who had finished a cold shower. She took the tall cold glass and sipped from it and then held it against the smooth dark skin of her belly. She touched the glass to the tips of each of her breasts so they came erect and then took a long sip and held the cold glass against her belly again. "This is wonderful," she said.

He kissed her and she said, "Oh, that's nice. I'd forgotten about that. I don't see any good reason why I should give that up. Do you?"

"No."

"Well, I haven't," she said. "I'm not going to turn you over to someone else prematurely. That was a silly idea."

"Get dressed and come on out," David said.

"No. I want to have fun with you like in the old days."

"How?"

"You know. To make you happy."

"How happy?"

"This."

"Be careful," he said.

"Please."

"All right, if you want."

"The way it was in Grau du Roi the first time it ever happened?"

"If you want."

"Thank you for giving me this time because—"

"Don't talk."

"It's just like Grau du Roi but it's lovelier because it's in the daytime and we love each other more because I'd gone away. Please let's be slow and slow and slow—"

"Yes slow."

"Are you—"

"Yes."

"Are you really?"

"Yes if you want."

"Oh I want so much and you are and I have. Please be slow and let me keep it."

"You have it."

"Yes I do. I do have it. Oh yes I do. I do. Please come now with me. Please can you now—"

They lay on the sheets and Catherine with her brown leg over his, touching his instep lightly with her toes, rested on her elbows and lifted her mouth from his and said, "Are you glad to have me back?"

"You," he said. "You did come back."

"You never thought I would. Yesterday it was all gone and everything was over and now here I am. Are you happy?"

"Yes."

"Do you remember when all I wanted was to be so dark and now I'm the darkest white girl in the world."

"And the blondest. You're just like ivory. That's how I always think. You're smooth as ivory too."

"I'm so happy and I want to have fun with you the way we always had. But mine is mine. I'm not going to turn you over to her the way I was doing and keep nothing. That's over."

"It's not awfully clear," David said. "But you really are fine again, aren't you?"

"I really am," Catherine said. "I'm not gloomy or morbid or pitiful."

"You're nice and lovely."

"It's all wonderful and changed. We're going to take turns," Catherine said. "You're mine today and tomorrow. And you're Marita's the next two days. My God, I'm hungry. This is the first time I've been hungry in a week."

When David and Catherine came back from swimming in the late afternoon they drove into Cannes for the Paris papers and then sat at the cafe and read and talked before they came home. After David had changed he found Marita sitting at the bar reading. He recognized the book as his own. The one she had not read. "Did you have a good swim?" she asked.

"Yes. We swam a long way out."

"Did you dive from the high rocks?"

"No."

"I'm glad of that," she said. "How is Catherine?"

"More cheerful."

"Yes. She is very intelligent."

"How are you? Are you all right?"

"Very well. I'm reading this book."

"How is it?"

"I can't tell you till day after tomorrow. I'm reading very slowly to make it last."

"What's that? The pact?"

"I suppose so. But I wouldn't worry very much about the book nor how I feel about you. It's not changed."

"All right," David said. "But I missed you very badly this morning."

"Day after tomorrow," she said. "Don't worry."

Chapter Twenty-one

THE NEXT DAY in the story was very bad because long before noon he knew that it was not just the need for sleep that made the difference between a boy and men. For the first three hours he was fresher than they were and he asked Juma for the .303 rifle to carry but Juma shook his head. He did not smile and he had always been David's best friend and had taught him to hunt. He offered it to me yesterday, David thought, and I'm in much better shape today than I was yesterday. He was too but by ten o'clock he knew the day would be bad or worse than the day before. It was as silly for him to think that he could trail with his father as to think he could fight with him. He knew too that it was not just that they were men. They were professional hunters and he knew now that was why Juma would not even waste a smile. They knew everything the elephant had done, pointed out the signs of it to each other without speaking, and when the tracking became difficult his father always yielded to Juma. When they stopped to fill the water bottles at a stream his father said, "Just last the day out, Davey." Then when they were finally past the broken country and climbing again toward the forest the tracks of the elephant turned off to the right onto an old elephant trail. He saw his father and Juma talking and when he got up to them Juma was looking back over the way they had come and then at a far distant stony island of hills in the dry country and seemed to be taking a bearing of this against the peaks of three far blue hills on the horizon.

"Juma knows where he's going now," his father explained. "He thought he knew before but then he dropped down into this stuff." He looked back at the country they had come through all day. "Where he's headed now is pretty good going but we'll have to climb."

They had climbed until it was dark and then made another dry camp. David had killed two spur fowl with his slingshot out of a small flock that had walked across the trail just before the sunset. The birds had come into the old elephant trail to dust, walking neatly and plumply, and when the pebble broke the back of one and the bird began to jerk and toss with its wings thumping, another bird ran forward to peck at it and David pouched another pebble and pulled it back and sent it against the ribs of the second bird. As he ran forward to put his hand on it the other birds whirred off. Juma had looked back and smiled this time and David picked up the two birds, warm and plump and smoothly feathered and knocked their heads against the handle of his hunting knife.

Now where they were camped for the night his father said, "I've never seen that type of Francolin quite so high. You did very well to get a double on them."

Juma cooked the birds spitted on a stick over the coals of a very small fire. His father drank a whiskey and water from the cup top of his flask as they lay and watched Juma cook. Afterward Juma gave them each a breast with the heart in it and ate the two necks and backs and the legs himself.

"It makes a great difference, Davey," his father said. "We're very well off on rations now."

"How far are we behind him?" David asked.

"We're quite close actually," his father said. "It all depends on whether he travels when the moon comes up. It's an hour later tonight and two hours later than when you found him."

"Why does Juma think he knows where he's going?"

"He wounded him and killed his *askari* not too far from here."

"When?"

"Five years ago, he says. That may mean anytime. When you were still a *toto* he says."

"Has he been alone since then?"

"He says so. He hasn't seen him. Only heard of him."

"How big does he say he is?"

"Close to two hundred. Bigger than anything I've ever seen. He says there's only been one greater elephant and he came from near here too."

"I'd better get to sleep," David said. "I hope I'll be better tomorrow."

"You were splendid today," his father said. "I was very proud of you. So was Juma."

In the night when he woke after the moon was up he was sure they were not proud of him except perhaps for his dexterity in killing the two birds. He had found the elephant at night and followed him to see that he had both of his tusks and then returned to find the two men and put them on the trail. David knew they were proud of that. But once the deadly following started he was useless to them and a danger to their success just as Kibo had been to him when he had gone up close to the elephant in the night, and he knew they must each have hated themselves for not having sent him back when there was time. The tusks of the elephant weighed two hundred pounds apiece. Ever since these tusks had grown beyond their normal size the elephant had been hunted for them and now the three of them would kill him. David was sure that they would kill him now because he, David, had lasted through the day and kept up after the pace had destroyed him by noon. So they probably were proud of him doing that. But he had brought nothing useful to the hunt and they would have been far better off without him. Many times during the day he had wished that he had never betrayed the elephant and in the afternoon he remembered wishing that he had never seen him. Awake in the moonlight he knew that was not true.

All morning, writing, he had been trying to remember truly how he felt and what had happened on that day. The hardest to make truly was how he had felt and keep it untinctured by how he had felt later. The details of the country were sharp and clear as the morning until the foreshortening and prolongation of exhaustion and he had written that well. But his feeling about the elephant had been the hardest part and he knew he would have to get away from it and then come back to it to be certain it was as it had been, not later, but on that day. He knew the feeling had begun to form but he had been too exhausted to remember it exactly.

Still involved in this problem and living in the story he locked up his suitcase and came out of the room onto the flagstones that led down to the terrace where Marita was sitting in a chair under one of the pines facing out toward the sea. She was reading and as he was walking barefooted she did not hear him. David looked at her and was pleased to see her. Then he remembered the preposterous situation and turned into the hotel and walked to his and Catherine's own room. She wasn't in the room and, still feeling Africa to be completely real and all of this where he was to be unreal and false, he went out on the terrace to speak to Marita.

"Good morning," he said. "Have you seen Catherine?"

"She went off somewhere," the girl said. "She said to tell you she'd be back."

Suddenly it was not unreal at all.

"You don't know where she went?"

"No," the girl said. "She went off on her bike."

"My God," David said. "She hasn't ridden a bike since we bought the Bug."

"That's what she said. She's taking it up again. Did you have a good morning?"

"I don't know. I'll know tomorrow."

"Are you eating breakfast?"

"I don't know. It's late."

"I wish you would."

"I'll go in and get cleaned up," he told her.

He had taken a shower and was shaving when Catherine came in. She was wearing an old Grau du Roi shirt and short linen slacks chopped off below the knees and she was hot and her shirt was wet through.

"It's wonderful," she said. "But I'd forgotten what it does to your upper thighs when you climb."

"Did you ride very far, Devil?"

"Six kilometers," she said. "It was nothing but I'd forgotten about the *côtes*."

"It's awfully hot to ride now unless you go in the very early mornings," David said. "I'm glad you started again though."

She was under the shower now and when she came out she said, "Now see how dark we are together. We're just the way we planned."

"You're darker."

"Not much. You're terribly dark too. Look at us together."

They looked at each other standing touching in the long mirror on the door.

"Oh you like us," she said. "That's nice. So do I. Touch here and see."

She stood very straight and he put his hand on her breasts.

"I'll put on one of my tight shirts so you can tell what I think about things," she said. "Isn't it funny our hair hasn't any color at all when it's wet? It's pale as seaweed."

She took a comb and combed her hair straight back so it looked as though she had just come out of the sea.

"I'm going to wear mine this way now again," she said. "Like Grau du Roi and here in the spring."

"I like it across your forehead."

"I'm tired of that. But I can do it if you like. Do you think we could go into town and have breakfast at the cafe?"

"Haven't you had breakfast?"

"I wanted to wait for you."

"All right," he said. "Let's go in and get breakfast. I'm hungry too."

They had a very good breakfast of café au lait, brioche and strawberry jam and *oeufs au plat avec jambon* and when they were finished Catherine asked, "Would you come over with me to Jean's? It's the day I go to get my hair washed and I'm going to have it cut."

"I'll wait here for you."

"Wouldn't you please come? You did it before and it wasn't bad for anybody."

"No, Devil. I did once but that was just once. Like getting tattooed or something. Don't ask me to."

"It doesn't mean anything except to me. I want us to be just the same."

"We can't be the same."

"Yes we could if you'd let us."

"I really don't want to do it."

"Not if I say it's all I want?"

"Why can't you want something that makes sense?"

"I do. But I want us to be the same and you almost are and it wouldn't be any trouble to do. The sea's done all the work."

"Then let the sea do it."

"I want it for today."

"Then you'll be happy I suppose."

"I'm happy now because you're going to do it and I'll stay happy. You love how I look. You know you do. Think of it that way."

"It's silly."

"No it isn't. Not when it's you and you do it to please me."

"How badly will you feel if I don't?"

"I don't know. But very."

"All right," he said. "It really means all that to you?"

"Yes," she said. "Oh, thank you. It won't take very long this time. I told Jean we'd be there and he's staying open for us."

"Are you always that confident I'll do things?"

"I knew you would if you knew how much I wanted it."

"I wanted very much not to. You shouldn't ask it."

"You won't care. It's nothing and afterwards it will be fun. Don't worry about Marita."

"What about her?"

"She said that if you wouldn't do it for me to ask you if you'd do it for her."

"Don't make things up."

"No. She said it this morning."

"I wish you could see yourself," Catherine said.

"I'm glad I can't."

"I wish you'd looked in the glass."

"I couldn't."

"Just look at me. That's how you are and I did it and there's nothing you can do now. That's how you look."

"We couldn't really have done that," David said. "I couldn't look the way you do."

"Well, we did," Catherine said. "And you do. So you better start to like it."

"We can't have done that, Devil."

"Yes we did. You knew it too. You just wouldn't look. And we're damned now. I was and now you are. Look at me and see how much you like it."

David looked at her eyes that he loved and at her dark face and the incredibly flat ivory color of her hair and at how happy she looked and he began to realize what a completely stupid thing he had permitted.

Chapter Twenty-two

HE DID NOT THINK that he could go on with the story that morning and for a long time he could not. But he knew that he must and finally he had started and they were following the spoor of the elephant on an old elephant trail that was a hard packed worn road through the forest. It looked as though elephants had travelled it ever since the lava had cooled from the mountain and the trees had first grown tall and close. Juma was very confident and they moved fast. Both his father and Juma seemed very sure of themselves and the going on the elephant road was so easy that Juma gave him the .303 to carry as they went on through the broken light of the forest. Then they lost the trail in smoking piles of fresh dung and the flat round prints of a herd of elephants that had come onto the elephant road from the heavy forest on the left of the trail. Juma had taken the .303 from David angrily. It was afternoon before they had worked up to the herd and around it seeing the gray bulks through the trees and the movement of the big ears and the searching trunks coiling and uncoiling, the crash of branches broken, the crash of trees pushed over and the rumbling in the bellies of the elephants and the slap and thud of the dung falling.

They had found the trail of the old bull finally and when it turned off onto a smaller elephant road Juma had looked at David's father and grinned showing his filed teeth and his father had nodded his head. They looked as though they had a dirty secret, just as they had looked when he had found them that night at the shamba.

It was not very long before they came on the secret. It was off to the right in the forest and the tracks of the old bull led to it. It was a skull as high as David's chest and white from the sun and the rains. There was a deep depression in the forehead and ridges ran from between the bare white eye sockets and flared out in empty broken holes where the tusks had been chopped away. Juma pointed out where the great elephant they were trailing had stood while he looked down at the skull and where his trunk had moved it a little way from the place it had rested on the ground and where the points of his tusks had touched the ground beside it. He showed David the single hole in the big depression in the white bone of forehead and then the four holes close together in the bone around the ear hole. He grinned at David and at his father and took a .303 solid from his pocket and fitted the nose into the hole in the bone of the forehead.

"Here is where Juma wounded the big bull," his father said. "This was his *askari*. His friend, really, because he was a big bull too. He charged and Juma knocked him down and finished him in the ear."

Juma was pointing out the scattered bones and how the big bull had walked around among them. Juma and David's father were both very pleased with what they had found.

"How long do you suppose he and his friend had been together?" David asked his father.

"I haven't the faintest idea," his father said. "Ask Juma."

"You ask him please."

His father and Juma spoke together and Juma had looked at David and laughed.

"Probably four or five times your life he says," David's father told him. "He doesn't know or care really."

I care, David thought. I saw him in the moonlight and he was alone but I had Kibo. Kibo has me too. The bull wasn't doing anyone any harm and now we've tracked him to where he came to see his dead friend and now we're going to kill him. It's my fault. I betrayed him.

Now Juma had worked out the trail and motioned to his father and they started on.

My father doesn't need to kill elephants to live, David thought. Juma would not have found him if I had not seen him. He had his chance at him and all he did was wound him and kill his friend. Kibo and I found him and I never should have told them and I should have kept him secret and had him always and let them stay drunk with their *bibis* at the beer shamba. Juma was so drunk we could not wake him. I'm going to keep everything a secret always. I'll never tell them anything again. If they kill him Juma will drink his share of the ivory or just buy himself another god damn wife. Why didn't you help the elephant when you could? All you had to do was not go on the second day. No, that wouldn't have stopped them. Juma would have gone on. You never should have told them. Never, never tell them. Try and remember that. Never tell anyone anything ever. Never tell anyone anything again.

His father waited for him to come up and said very gently, "He rested here. He's not travelling as he was. We'll be up on him anytime now."

"Fuck elephant hunting," David had said very quietly.

"What's that?" his father asked.

"Fuck elephant hunting," David said softly.

"Be careful you don't fuck it up," his father had said to him and looked at him flatly.

That's one thing, David had thought. He's not stupid. He knows all about it now and he will never trust me again. That's good. I don't want him to because I'll never ever tell him or anybody anything again never anything again. Never ever never.

That was where he stopped in the hunt that morning. He knew he did not have it right yet. He had not gotten the enormity of the skull as they had come onto it in the forest nor the tunnels underneath it in the earth that the beetles had made and that had been revealed like deserted galleries or catacombs when the elephant had moved the skull. He had not made the great length of the whitened bones nor how the elephant's tracks had moved around the scene of the killing and how following them he had been able to see the elephant as he had moved and then had been able to see what the elephant had seen. He had not gotten the great width of the one elephant trail that was a perfect road through the forest nor the worn smooth rubbing trees nor the way other trails intersected so that they were like the map of the Métro in Paris. He had not made the light in the forest where the trees came together at their tops and he had not clarified certain things that he must make as they were then, not as he recalled them now. The distances did not matter since all distances changed and how you remembered them was how they were. But his change of feeling toward Juma and toward his father and toward the elephant was complicated by the exhaustion that had bred it. Tiredness brought the beginning of understanding. The understanding was beginning and he was realizing it as he wrote. But the dreadful true understanding was all to come and he must not show it by arbitrary statements of rhetoric but by remembering the actual things that had brought it. Tomorrow he would get the things right and then go on.

He put the cahiers of manuscript away in the suitcase and

locked it and came out the door of his room and walked along the front of the hotel to where Marita was reading.

"Do you want breakfast?" she asked.

"I think I'd like a drink."

"Let's have it at the bar," she said. "It's cooler."

They went in and sat down on stools and David poured from the Haig Pinch bottle into a glass and filled it up with cold Perrier.

"What became of Catherine?"

"She left very happy and gay."

"And how are you?"

"Happy and shy and rather quiet."

"Too shy for me to kiss you?"

They held each other and he could feel himself start to be whole again. He had not known just how greatly he had been divided and separated because once he started to work he wrote from an inner core which could not be split nor even marked nor scratched. He knew about this and it was his strength since all the rest of him could be riven.

They sat at the bar while the boy laid the table and the first coolness of fall was in the breeze from the sea and then sitting at the table under the pines they felt it again as they ate and drank.

"This cool breeze comes all the way from Kurdistan," David said. "The equinoctial storms will be coming soon."

"They won't come today," the girl said. "We don't have to worry about them today."

"There hasn't been a blow of any kind since when we met in Cannes at the cafe."

"Can you still remember things that long ago?"

"It seems further away than the war."

"I had the war the last three days," the girl said. "I just left it this morning."

"I never think about it," David said.

"Now I've read it," Marita told him, "but I don't understand about you. You never made clear what you believed."

He filled her glass and then refilled his own.

"I didn't know until afterwards," he said. "So I didn't try to act as though I did. I suspended thinking about it while it was happening. I only felt and saw and acted and thought tactically. That's why it's not a better book. Because I wasn't more intelligent."

"It is a very good book. The flying parts are wonderful and the feeling for the other people and for the planes themselves."

"I'm good on other people and on technical and tactical things," David said. "I don't mean to talk wet or to brag. But, Marita, nobody knows about himself when he is really involved. Yourself isn't worth considering. It would be shameful at the time."

"But afterwards you know."

"Sure. Sometimes."

"Can I read the narrative?"

David poured wine in the glasses again.

"How much did she tell you?"

"She said she told me everything. She tells things very well you know."

"I'd rather you didn't read it," David said. "All it would do is make trouble. I didn't know there would be you when I wrote it and I can't help her telling you things but I don't have to have you read about them too."

"Then I mustn't read it?"

"I wish you wouldn't. I don't want to give you orders."

"Then I have to tell you," the girl said.

"She let you read it?"

"Yes. She said I should."

"God damn her."

"She didn't do it to do wrong. It was when she was so worried."

"So you read it all?"

"Yes. It's wonderful. It's so much better than the last book and now the stories are so much better than it or than anything."

"What about the Madrid part?" He looked at her and she looked up at him and then moistened her lips and did not look away and she said very carefully, "I knew all about that because I'm just the way you are."

When they were lying together Marita said, "You don't think about her when you make love to me?"

"No, stupid."

"You don't want me to do her things? Because I know them all and I can do them."

"Stop talking and just feel."

"I can do them better than she can."

"Stop talking."

"Don't think you have to—"

"Don't talk."

"But you don't have to—"

"No one has to but we are—"

They lay holding each other close and hard and then gently finally and Marita said, "I have to go away but I'll be back. Please sleep for me."

She kissed him and when she came back he was asleep. He had meant to wait for her but he had fallen asleep while he waited. She lay down by him and kissed him and when he did not wake she lay by him very quietly and tried to sleep too. But she was not sleepy and she kissed him very softly again and then commenced to play with him very gently while she pushed her breasts against him. He stirred in his sleep and she lay now with her head down below his chest and played softly and searchingly making small intimacies and discoveries.

It was a long cool afternoon and David slept and when he

woke Marita was gone and he heard the two girls' voices on the terrace. He dressed and unbolted the door to his working room and then came out from the door of that room onto the flag-stones. There was no one on the terrace except the waiter who was taking in the tea things and he found the girls in the bar.

Chapter Twenty-three

THE TWO GIRLS were both sitting at the bar with a bottle of Perrier-Jouët in a bucket with ice and they both looked fresh and lovely.

"It's just like meeting an ex-husband," Catherine said. "It makes me feel very sophisticated." She had never looked gayer or more lovely. "I must say it agrees with you." She looked at David in mock appraisal.

"Do you think he's all right?" Marita said. She looked at David and blushed.

"And well you might blush," Catherine said. "Look at her, David."

"She looks very well," David said. "So do you."

"She looks about sixteen," Catherine said. "She said she told you about reading the narrative."

"I think you should have asked me," David said.

"I know I should," Catherine said. "But I started to read it for myself and then it was so interesting I thought Heiress ought to read it too."

"I'd have said no."

"But the point is," Catherine said, "if he ever says no about anything, Marita, just keep right on. It doesn't mean a thing."

"I don't believe it," Marita said. She smiled at David.

"That's because he hasn't written the narrative up to date. When he does you'll find out."

"I'm through with the narrative," David said.

"That's dirty," Catherine said. "That was my present and our project."

"You must write it, David," the girl said. "You will won't you?"

"She wants to be in it, David," Catherine said. "And it will be so much better when you have a dark girl too."

David poured himself a glass of the champagne. He saw Marita look at him, a warning, and he said to Catherine, "I'll go on with it when I finish the stories. What did you do with your day?"

"I had a fine day. I made decisions and planned things."

"Oh God," David said.

"They're all straightforward plans," Catherine said. "You don't have to groan about them. You've been doing just whatever you wanted to do all day and I was pleased. But I have a right to make a few plans."

"What sort of plans?" David asked. His voice sounded very flat.

"First we have to start seeing about getting the book out. I'm going to have to have the manuscript typed up to where it is now and see about getting illustrations. I have to see the artists and make the arrangements."

"You've had a very busy day," David said. "You know, don't you, that you don't get manuscripts typed until whoever writes them has gone over them and has them ready for typing?"

"That isn't necessary because I only need a rough draft to show the artists."

"I see. And if I don't want it copied yet?"

"Don't you want it brought out? I do. And someone has to get started on something practical."

"Who are the artists you thought up today?"

"Different ones for different parts. Marie Laurencin, Pascen, Derain, Dufy and Picasso."

"For Christ sake, Derain."

"Can't you see a nice Laurencin of Marita and me in the car when we stopped the first time by the Loup on the way to Nice?"

"Nobody's written that."

"Well write it then. It's certainly much more interesting and instructive than a lot of natives in a kraal or whatever you call it covered with flies and scabs in Central Africa with your drunken father staggering around smelling of sour beer and not knowing which ones of the little horrors he had fathered."

"There goes the ball game," David said.

"What did you say, David?" Marita said.

"I said thank you very much for having lunch with me," David told her.

"Why don't you thank her for the rest of it?" Catherine said. "She really must have done something impressive to make you sleep as though you were dead until the absolute end of the afternoon. Thank her for that at least."

"Thank you for going swimming," David said to the girl.

"Oh did you swim?" Catherine said. "I'm glad you swam."

"We swam quite far," Marita said. "And we had a very good lunch. Did you have a good lunch, Catherine?"

"I think so," Catherine said. "I don't remember."

"Where were you?" Marita asked gently.

"Saint Raphael," Catherine said. "I remember stopping there but I can't remember about lunch. I never notice when I eat by myself. But I'm quite sure I did have lunch there. I know I intended to."

"Was it nice driving back?" Marita asked. "It was such a cool lovely afternoon."

"I don't know," Catherine said. "I didn't notice. I was thinking about making the book and getting it started. We have to get it started. I don't know why David started to be difficult the moment I commenced to put a little order into it. The whole thing has dragged along in such a haphazard way that I was suddenly ashamed of all of us."

"Poor Catherine," Marita said. "But now that you have it all planned you must feel better."

"I do," Catherine said. "I felt so happy when I came in. I knew I'd made you happy and I'd accomplished something practical too and then David made me feel like an idiot or a leper. I can't help it if I'm practical and sensible."

"I know, Devil," David said. "I just didn't want to get the work mixed up."

"But it's you who mixed it up," Catherine said. "Can't you see? Jumping back and forth trying to write stories when all you had to do was keep on with the narrative that meant so much to all of us. It was going so well too and we were just coming to the most exciting parts. Someone has to show you that the stories are just your way of escaping your duty."

Marita looked at him again and he knew what she was trying to tell him and he said, "I have to go get cleaned up. You tell Marita about it and I'll be back."

"We have other things to talk about," Catherine said. "I'm sorry I was rude about you and Marita. I couldn't be happier about you really."

David took everything that had been said in with him to the bathroom where he had a shower and changed into a newly washed fisherman's sweater and slacks. It was quite cool now in the evening and Marita was sitting at the bar looking at *Vogue*.

"She's gone down to see about your room," Marita said.

"How is she?"

"How should I know, David? She's a very great publisher now. She's given up sex. It doesn't interest her anymore. It's childish really, she says. She doesn't know how it could ever have meant anything to her. But she may decide to have an affair with another woman if she ever takes it up again. There's quite a bit about another woman."

"Christ I never thought it would go this way."

"Don't," Marita said. "No matter what or how it is I love you and you are going to write tomorrow."

Catherine came in and said, "You look wonderful together and I'm so proud. I feel as though I'd invented you. Was he good today, Marita?"

"We had a nice lunch," Marita said. "Please be fair, Catherine."

"Oh I know he's a satisfactory lover," Catherine said. "He's always that. That's just like his martinis or how he swims or skis or flew probably. I never saw him with a plane. Everyone says he was marvelous. It's like acrobats really I suppose and just as dull. I wasn't asking about that."

"You were very good to let us spend a day together, Catherine," Marita said.

"You can spend the rest of your lives together," Catherine said. "If you don't bore each other. I have no further need of either of you."

David was watching her in the mirror and she looked calm, handsome and normal. He could see Marita looking at her very sadly.

"I do like to look at you though and I'd like to hear you talk if you'd ever open your mouths."

"How do you do," said David.

"That was quite a good effort," Catherine said. "I'm very well."

"Have any new plans?" David asked. He felt as though he were hailing a ship.

"Only what I've told you," Catherine went on. "They'll probably keep me quite busy."

"What was all the guff about another woman?"

He felt Marita kick him and he put his foot on hers to acknowledge.

"That's not guff," Catherine said. "I want to have one more try to see if I've missed anything. I might have."

"All of us are fallible," David said and Marita kicked him again.

"I want to see," Catherine said. "I know enough about that now so I should be able to tell. Don't worry about your dark girl. She's not my type at all. She's yours. She's what you like and very nice it is but not for me. I'm not attracted to the gamin type."

"Perhaps I am a gamin," Marita said.

"That's a very polite word for that part."

"But I'm also more of a woman than you are Catherine."

"Go ahead and show David what sort of gamin you are. He'd like it."

"He knows what sort of woman I am."

"That's splendid," Catherine said. "I'm glad you both found your tongues finally. I do prefer conversation."

"You aren't really a woman at all," Marita said.

"I know it," Catherine said. "I've tried to explain it to David often enough. Isn't that true, David?"

David looked at her and said nothing.

"Didn't I?"

"Yes," he said.

"I did try and I broke myself in pieces in Madrid to be a girl and all it did was break me in pieces," Catherine said. "Now all I am is through. You're a girl and a boy both and you really are. You don't have to change and it doesn't kill you and I'm not. And now I'm nothing. All I wanted was for David and you to be happy. Everything else I invent."

Marita said, "I know it and I try to tell David."

"I know you do. But you don't have to be loyal to me or to anything. Don't do it. Nobody would anyway and you probably aren't really. But I tell you not to be. I want you to be happy and make him happy. You can too and I can't and I know it."

"You're the finest girl there is," Marita said.

"I'm not. I'm finished before I ever started."

"No. I'm the one," Marita said. "I was stupid and awful."

"You weren't stupid. Everything you said was true. Let's stop talking and be friends. Can we?"

"Can we please?" Marita asked her.

"I want to," Catherine said. "And not be such a tragic bully. Please take your time about the book, David. You know all I want is for you to write the best you can. That's what we started with. I'm over it now whatever this one was."

"You were just tired," David said. "I don't think you ate any lunch either."

"Probably not," Catherine said. "But I may have. Can we forget it all now though and just be friends?"

So they were friends; whatever friends are, David thought, and tried not to think but talked and listened in the unreality that reality had become. He had heard each one speak about the other and he knew each must know what the other thought and probably what they each had told him. In that way they really were friends, understanding in their basic disagreement, trusting in their complete distrust and enjoying one another's company. He enjoyed their company too but tonight he'd had enough of it.

Tomorrow he must go back into his own country, the one that Catherine was jealous of and that Marita loved and respected. He had been happy in the country of the story and knew that it was too good to last and now he was back from what he cared about into the overpopulated vacancy of madness that had taken, now, the new turn of exaggerated practicality. He was tired of it and he was tired of Marita's collaborating with her enemy. Catherine was not his enemy except as she was himself in the unfinding unrealizable quest that is love and so was her own enemy. She needs an enemy so badly always that she has to keep one near and she's the nearest and the easiest to attack knowing the weaknesses and strengths and all the faults of our defenses. She turns my flank so skillfully then finds it is her own and the last fighting is always in a swirl and the dust that rises is our own dust.

Catherine wanted to play backgammon with Marita after dinner. They always played it seriously and for money and when Catherine went to get the board Marita said to David, "Please don't come to my room tonight after all."

"Good."

"Do you understand?"

"Let's skip that word," David said. His coldness had come back as the time for working moved closer.

"Are you angry?"

"Yes," David said.

"At me?"

"No."

"You can't be angry with someone who's ill."

"You haven't lived very long," David said. "That's exactly who everyone is always angry with. Get ill sometime yourself and see."

"I wish you wouldn't be angry."

"I wish I'd never seen any of you."

"Please don't, David."

"You know it isn't true. I'm only getting ready to work."

He went into their bedroom and put on the reading light on his side of the bed and made himself comfortable and read one of the W. H. Hudson books. It was *Nature in Downland* and he had taken it to read because it had the most unpromising title. He knew enough to know a time was coming when he'd need all the books and he was saving the best ones. But once past the title of this one nothing in it bored him. He was happy to read and he was back out of his life and with Hudson and his brother riding their horses into the tumbled whiteness of breast-high thistledown in the moonlight and gradually the click of dice and the low sound of the girls' voices became real again too so that when, after a time, he went out to make himself a whiskey and Perrier to take back to his reading they seemed, when he saw them playing, to be actual human beings doing something normal and not figures in some unbelievable play he had been brought unwillingly to attend.

He went back to the room and read and drank his whiskey and Perrier very slowly and he had undressed and turned the light off and was almost asleep when he heard Catherine come in to the bedroom. It seemed to him that she was gone a long time in the bathroom before he felt her come to bed and he lay still and breathed steadily and hoped he might really go to sleep.

"Are you awake, David?" she asked.

"I think so."

"Don't wake up," she said. "Thank you for sleeping here."

"I usually do."

"You don't have to."

"Yes I do."

"I'm glad you did. Good night."

"Good night."

"Would you kiss me good night?"

"Sure," he said.

He kissed her and it was Catherine as she had been before when she had seemed to come back to him for a while.

"I'm sorry I was such a failure again."

"Let's not talk about things."

"Do you hate me?"

"No."

"Can we start again the way I'd planned things?"

"I don't think so."

"Then why did you come in here?"

"This is where I belong."

"No other reason?"

"I thought you might be lonely."

"I was."

"Everybody's lonely," David said.

"It's terrible to be in bed together and be lonely."

"There isn't any solution," David said. "All your plans and schemes are worthless."

"I didn't give it a chance."

"It was all crazy anyway. I'm sick of crazy things. You're not the only one gets broken up."

"I know. But can't we try it again just once more and I really be good? I can. I nearly was."

"I'm sick of all of it, Devil. Sick all the way through me."

"Wouldn't you try it just once more for her and for me both?"

"It doesn't work and I'm sick of it."

"She said you had a fine day and that you were really cheerful and not depressed. Won't you try it once more for both of us? I want it so much."

"You want everything so much and when you get it it's over and you don't give a damn."

"I was just overconfident this time and then I get insufferable. Please can we try it again?"

"Let's go to sleep, Devil, and not talk about it."

"Kiss me again please," Catherine said. "I'll go to sleep because I know you'll do it. You always do everything I want because you really want to do it too."

"You only want things for you, Devil."

"That's not true, David. Anyway I am you and her. That's what I did it for. I'm everybody. You know about that don't you?"

"Go to sleep, Devil."

"I will. But would you please kiss me again first so that we won't be lonely?"

Chapter Twenty-four

IN THE MORNING he was on the far slope of the mountain again. The elephant was no longer travelling as he had been but was moving aimlessly now, feeding occasionally and David had known they were getting close to him. He tried to remember how he had felt. He had no love for the elephant yet. He must remember that. He had only a sorrow that had come from his own tiredness that had brought an understanding of age. Though being too young, he had learned how it must be to be too old. He was lonesome for Kibo and thinking of Juma killing the elephant's friend had turned him against Juma and made the elephant his brother. He knew then how much it meant to him to have seen the elephant in the moonlight and for him to have followed him with Kibo and come close to him in the clearing so that he had seen both of the great tusks. But he did not know that nothing would ever be as good as that again. Now he knew they would kill the elephant and there was nothing he could do about it. He had betrayed the elephant when he had gone back to tell them at the shamba. They would kill me and they would kill Kibo too if we had ivory, he had thought and known it was untrue. Probably the elephant is going to find where he was born now and they'll kill him there. That's all they'd need to make it perfect. They'd like to have killed him where they killed his friend. That would be a big joke. That would have pleased them. The god damned friend killers.

They had moved to the edge of thick cover now and the elephant was close ahead. David could smell him and they could all hear him pulling down branches and the snapping that they made. His father put his hand on David's shoulder to move him back and have him wait outside and then he took a big pinch of ashes from the pouch in his pocket and tossed it in the air. The ash barely slanted toward them as it fell and his father nodded at Juma and bent down to follow him into the thick cover. David watched their backs and their asses go in and out of sight. He could not hear them move.

David had stood still and listened to the elephant feeding. He could smell him as strongly as he had the night in the moonlight when he had worked up close to him and had seen his wonderful tusks. Then as he stood there it was silent and he could not smell the elephant. Then there had been a high squealing and smashing and a shot by the .303 then the heavy rocking double report of his father's .450, then the smashing and crashing had gone on going steadily away and he had gone into the heavy growth and found Juma standing shaken and bleeding from his forehead all down over his face and his father white and angry.

"He went for Juma and knocked him over," his father had said. "Juma hit him in the head."

"Where did you hit him?"

"Where I fucking well could," his father had said. "Get on the fucking blood spoor."

There was plenty of blood. One stream as high as David's head that had squirted bright on trunks and leaves and vines and another much lower that was dark and foul with stomach content.

"Lung and gut shot," his father said. "We'll find him down or anchored—I hope the hell," he added.

They found him anchored, in such suffering and despair that he could no longer move. He had crashed through the heavy cover where he had been feeding and crossed a path of open forest and David and his father had run along the heavily splashed blood trail. Then the elephant had gone on into thick forest and David had seen him ahead standing gray and huge against the trunk of a tree. David could only see his stern and then his father moved ahead of him and he followed and they came alongside the elephant as though he was a ship and David saw the blood coming from his flanks and running down his sides and then his father raised his rifle and fired and the elephant turned his head with the great tusks moving heavy and slow and looked at them and when his father fired the second barrel the elephant seemed to sway like a felled tree and came smashing down toward them. But he was not dead. He had been anchored and now he was down with his shoulder broken. He did not move but his eye was alive and looked at David. He had very long eyelashes and his eye was the most alive thing David had ever seen.

"Shoot him in the ear hole with the three oh three," his father said. "Go on."

"You shoot him," David had said.

Juma had come up limping and bloody, the skin of his forehead hanging down over his left eye, the bone of his nose showing and one ear torn and had taken the rifle from David without speaking and pushed the muzzle almost into the ear hole and fired twice jerking the bolt and driving it forward angrily. The eye of the elephant had opened wide on the first shot and then started to glaze and blood came out of the ear and ran in two bright streams down the wrinkled gray hide. It was a different colored blood and David had thought I must remember that and he had but it had never been of any use to him. Now all the dignity and majesty and all the beauty was gone from the elephant and he was a huge wrinkled pile.

"Well we got him, Davey, thanks to you," his father had said. "Now we'd better get a fire going so I can put Juma back together again. Come here you bloody Humpty Dumpty. Those tusks will keep."

Juma had come to him grinning bringing the tail of the elephant that had no hairs on it at all. They had made a dirty joke and then his father had begun to speak rapidly in Swahili: How far to water? How far will you have to go to get people to get those tusks out of here? How are you, you worthless old pig fucker? What have you broken?

Then with the answers known his father had said, "You and I will go back to get the packs where we dropped them when we went in after him. Juma can get wood and have the fire ready. The medical kit is in my pack. We have to get the packs before it's dark. He won't infect. It's not like claw wounds. Let's go."

His father had known how he had felt about the elephant and that night and in the next few days he had tried if not to convert him to bring him back to the boy he had been before he had come to the knowledge that he hated elephant hunting. David had put no statement of his father's intention, which had never been stated, in the story but had only used the happenings, the disgusts, the events and feelings of the butchering, and the work of chopping out the tusks and of the rough surgery on Juma disguised by mockery and railery to keep the pain in contempt and reduce its stature since there were no drugs. The added responsibility David was given and the trust that was offered him and not accepted he had put in the story without pointing their significance. He had tried to make the elephant alive beneath the tree anchored in his final anguish and drowning in the blood that had flowed so many times before but always staunched and now was rising in him so he could not breathe, the great heart pumping it to drown him as he watched the man who came to finish him. David had been so proud the elephant had scented Juma and charged him instantly. He would have killed Juma if his father had not fired into him so that he had thrown Juma into the trees with his trunk and charged on with the death in him, feeling it as only another wound until the blood welled up and he could not breathe against it. That evening as David had sat by the fire he had looked at Juma with his stitched up face and his broken ribs that he tried to breathe without and wondered if the elephant had recognized him when he had tried to kill him. He hoped he had. The elephant was his hero now as his father had been for a long time and he had thought, I did not believe he could do it when he was so old and tired. He would have killed Juma too. But he didn't look at me as though he wanted to kill me. He only looked sad the same way I felt. He visited his old friend on the day he died.

It was a very young boy's story, he knew, when he had finished it. He read it over and saw the gaps he must fill in to make it so that whoever read it would feel it was truly happening as it was read and he marked the gaps in the margin.

He remembered how the elephant lost all dignity as soon as his eye had ceased to be alive and how when his father and he had returned with the packs the elephant had already started to swell even in the cool evening. There was no more true elephant, only the gray wrinkled swelling dead body and the huge great mottled brown and yellow tusks that they had killed him for. The tusks were stained with the dried blood and he scraped some of it off with his thumbnail like a dried piece of sealing wax and put it in the pocket of his shirt. That was all he took from the elephant except the beginning of the knowledge of loneliness.

After the butchery his father tried to talk to him that night by the fire.

"He was a murderer you know, Davey," he had said. "Juma says nobody knows how many people he has killed."

"They were all trying to kill him weren't they?"

"Naturally," his father had said, "with that pair of tusks."

"How could he be a murderer then?"

"Just as you like," his father had said. "I'm sorry you got so mixed up about him."

"I wish he'd killed Juma," David had said.

"I think that's carrying it a little far," his father said. "Juma's your friend you know."

"Not anymore."

"No need to tell him so."

"He knows it," David had said.

"I think you misjudge him," his father said and they had left it there.

Then when they were finally back safely with the tusks after all the things that had happened and the tusks were propped against the wall of the stick and mud house leaning there with their points touching, the tusks so tall and thick that no one could believe them even when they touched them and no one, not even his father, could reach to the top of the bend where they curved in for the points to meet, there when Juma and his father and he were heroes and Kibo was a hero's dog, and the men who had carried the tusks were heroes, already slightly drunk heroes and to be drunker, his father had said, "Do you want to make peace Davey?"

"All right," he said because he knew this was the start of the never telling that he had decided on.

"I'm so glad," his father said. "It's so much simpler and better."

Then they sat on old men's stools under the shade of the great fig tree with the tusks against the wall of the hut and drank native beer from gourd cups that were brought by a young girl and her younger brother, no longer a detested nuisance but the servant of heroes, sitting in the dust by the heroic dog of a hero who held an old cockerel newly promoted to the standing of the heroes' favorite rooster. They sat there and drank beer while the big drum started and the Ngoma began to build.

He came out of the working room and he was happy and empty and proud and Marita was waiting for him on the terrace sitting in the sun of the bright early fall morning that he had not known existed. It was a perfect morning, still and cool. The sea below was a flat calm and across the bay was the white curve of Cannes with the dark mountains behind it.

"I love you very much," he said to the dark girl as she stood up. He put his arms around her and kissed her and she said, "You finished it."

"Sure," he said. "Why not?"

"I love you and I'm so proud," she said. They walked out and looked at the sea with their arms around each other.

"How are you girl?"

"I'm very well and very happy," Marita said. "Did you mean it about loving me or was it just the morning?"

"It was the morning," David said and kissed her again.

"Can I read the story?"

"It's too lovely a day."

"Can't I read it so I can feel like you do and not just happy because you're happy like I was your dog?"

He gave her the key and when she brought the notebooks and read the story at the bar David read it sitting beside her. He knew it was ill mannered and stupid. He had never done this before with anyone and it was against everything he believed about writing but he did not think of that except at the moment when he put his arm around the girl and looked at the writing on the lined paper. He could not help wanting to read it with her and he could not help sharing what he had never shared and what he had believed could not and should not be shared.

When she finished reading Marita put her arms around David and kissed him so hard that she drew blood from his lip. He looked at her and tasted his blood absentmindedly and smiled.

"I'm sorry David," she said. "Please forgive me. I'm so very happy and prouder than you are."

"Is it all right?" he said. "Can you smell the shamba smell and the clean smell of hut inside and feel the smoothness of the old men chairs? It's really clean in the hut and the earth floor is swept."

"Of course it is. You had it in the other story. I can see the angle of the head of Kibo the heroic dog too. You were such a lovely hero. Did the blood make a stain in your pocket?"

"Yes. It softened when I sweated."

"Let's go to town and celebrate the day," Marita said. "There's a lot of things that we can do today."

David stopped at the bar and poured Haig Pinch and then cold Perrier into a glass and brought it with him to the room where he drank half of it and took a cold shower. Then he pulled on slacks and a shirt and put on *alpargatas* to go into town. He felt the story was good and felt even better about Marita. Neither had been diminished by the sharpening of perception he had now, and clarity had come with no sadness.

Catherine was doing whatever she was doing and would do whatever she would do. He looked out and felt the old happy carelessness. It was a day for flying actually. He wished there was a field where he could rent a plane and take Marita up and show her what you could do with a day like this. She might like it. But there isn't any field here. So forget that. It would be fun though. So would skiing. That's only two months away if you want it. Christ, it was good to finish today and have her there. Marita there with no damned jealousy of the work and have her know what you were reaching for and how far you went. She really knows and it's not faked. I do love her and you make a note of it, whiskey, and you witness it for me, Perrier old boy old Perrier, I have been faithful to you, Perrier, in my fucking fashion. It feels very good when you feel so good. It's a stupid feeling but it fits on this day so put it on.

"Come on girl," he said to Marita at the door of her room. "What's holding you up besides your beautiful legs?"

"I'm ready, David," she said. She had on a tight sweater and slacks and her face was shining. She brushed her dark hair and looked at him.

"It's wonderful when you're so gay."

"It's such a good day," he said. "And we're so lucky."

"Do you think so?" she said as they walked to the car. "Do you think we're really lucky?"

"Yes," he said. "I think it changed this morning or maybe in the night."

BOOK FOUR

Chapter Twenty-five

CATHERINE'S CAR was in the driveway of the hotel when they drove up. It was parked on the right side of the gravelled approach. David stopped the Isotta behind it and he and Marita got out and walked down the drive past the small, low empty blue car and onto the flagstones of the walk without speaking.

They passed David's room with the locked door and the open windows and Marita stopped outside of her door and said, "Goodbye."

"What are you doing this afternoon?" he asked.

"I don't know," she said. "I'll be here."

He walked on down to the patio of the hotel and went in the main door. Catherine was sitting at the bar reading the Paris *Herald* with a glass and half a bottle of wine beside her on the bar. She looked up at him.

"What brought you back?" she asked.

"We had lunch in town and came on up," David said.

"How is your whore?"

"I haven't one yet."

"I mean the one you write the stories for."

"Oh. The stories."

"Yes. The stories. The dreary dismal little stories about your adolescence with your bogus drunken father."

"He wasn't so bogus really."

"Didn't he defraud his wife and all his friends?"

"No. Just himself really."

"You certainly make him despicable in these last sketches or vignettes or pointless anecdotes you write about him."

"You mean the stories."

"You call them stories," Catherine said.

"Yes," David said and poured a glass of the lovely cold wine on the bright clear day in the pleasant, sunny room in the clean, comfortable hotel and, sipping it, felt it fail to lift up his dead cold heart.

"Would you like me to go and get Heiress?" Catherine said. "It wouldn't do to have her think that we'd had a misunderstanding about whose day it is or that we'd taken up solitary drinking together."

"You don't need to get her."

"I'd like to. She took care of you today and I didn't. Really, David, I'm not a bitch yet. I just act and talk like one."

While David waited for Catherine to come back he drank another glass of the champagne and read the Paris edition of *The New York Herald* she had left on the bar. Drinking the wine by himself it did not taste the same and he found a cork in the kitchen to stop up the bottle before he put it back in the ice chest. But the bottle did not feel heavy enough and lifting it against the light that came in the west window he saw how little wine was left and he poured it out and drank it off and put the bottle down on the tiled floor. Even when he drank it off quickly it did nothing for him.

Thank God he was breaking through on the stories now. What had made the last book good was the people who were in it and the accuracy of the detail which made it believable. He had, really, only to remember accurately and the form came by what he would choose to leave out. Then, of course, he could close it like the diaphragm of a camera and intensify it so it could be concentrated to the point where the heat shone bright and the smoke began to rise. He knew that he was getting this now.

What Catherine had said about the stories when she was trying to hurt him had started him thinking about his father and all the things he had tried to do whatever he could about. Now, he told himself, you must try to grow up again and face what you have to face without being irritable or hurt that someone did not understand and appreciate what you wrote. She understands it less and less. But you've worked well and nothing can touch you as long as you can work. Try to help her now and forget about yourself. Tomorrow you have the story to go over and to make perfect.

But David did not want to think about the story. He cared about the writing more than about anything else, and he cared about many things, but he knew that when he was doing it he must not worry about it nor finger it nor handle it any more than he would open up the door of the darkroom to see how a negative was developing. Leave it alone, he told himself. You are a bloody fool but you know that much.

His thoughts turned to the two girls and he wondered if he should go find them and see what they wanted to do or if they wanted to go off and swim. After all, it was Marita's and his day and she might be waiting. Maybe something could still be salvaged out of the day for all of them. They might be cooking something up. He ought to go by and ask what they wanted to do. Then do it, he told himself. Don't stand here and think about it. Go on and find them.

The door to Marita's room was shut and he knocked on it.

They had been talking and when he knocked the talking stopped.

"Who is it?" Marita asked.

He heard Catherine laugh and she said, "Come in whoever you are."

He heard Marita say something to her and Catherine said, "Come in, David."

He opened the door. They were lying in the big bed together side by side; the sheet pulled up under their chins.

"Please come in, David," Catherine said. "We've been waiting for you."

David looked at them, the serious dark girl and the fair laughing one. Marita looked at him trying to tell him something. Catherine was laughing.

"Won't you come in too, David?"

"I came by to see if you wanted to go to swim or anything," David said.

"I don't want to," Catherine said. "Heiress was in bed asleep and I got into bed with her. She was very good and asked me to leave. She's not a bit unfaithful to you. Not in the least little bit. But won't you come in too so we can both be faithful to you?"

"No," David said.

"Please, David," Catherine said. "It's such a lovely day."

"Do you want to go to swim?" David asked Marita.

"I'd like to," the girl said above the sheet.

"You two puritans," Catherine said. "Please both be reasonable and come to bed David."

"I want to go to swim," Marita said. "Please go out, David."

"Why can't he see you?" Catherine asked. "He sees you at the beach."

"He'll see me at the cove," Marita said. "Please go out, David."

David went out and closed the door without looking back, hearing Marita talking in a low voice to Catherine and Catherine's laughter. He walked down the flagstones to the front of the hotel and looked out at the sea. There was a light breeze now and he watched three French destroyers and a cruiser, neat and dark, and sharply etched on the blue sea as they moved in formation working out some problems. They were far out and they looked to be recognition silhouettes from their size until a white line would show at the bow as a ship speeded up to change the pattern. David watched them until the two girls came up to him.

"Please don't be cross," Catherine said.

They were dressed to go to the beach and Catherine put a bag with the towels and the robes on an iron chair.

"Are you going swimming too?" David said to her.

"If you're not angry with me."

David said nothing and watched the ships as they changed course and another destroyer moved out of the pattern at a sharp angle with the line of white curling back from her bows. She began to make smoke and it trailed in a black widening plume as she curved at flank speed.

"It was only a joke," Catherine said. "We'd been making such good rough jokes. You and I had."

"What are they doing, David?" Marita asked.

"Anti-sub maneuvers, I think," he said. "Maybe there are subs working with them. They're probably out from Toulon."

"They were in Sainte Maxime or Saint Raphael," Catherine said. "I saw them the other day."

"I don't know what it is now with the smoke screen," David said. "There must be other ships we can't see."

"There come the planes," Marita said. "Aren't they lovely?"

They were very small, neat sea-planes and three of them were coming around the point low over the water.

"When we were here in the early summer they had gunnery practice off the Porquerolles and it was terrific," Catherine said. "It shook the window. Will they use depth bombs now, David?"

"I don't know. I shouldn't think so if they're working with real subs."

"I can go to swim, can't I please David?" Catherine asked. "I'm going away and then you can swim all the time by yourselves."

"I asked you to swim," David said.

"That's true," Catherine said. "You did. Then let's go now and all be friends and happy. If the planes come in close they can see us on the beach at the cove and that will cheer them up."

The planes did come by close off the cove while David and Marita were swimming far out and Catherine was tanning on the beach. They passed rapidly, three echelons of three, their big Rhône motors roaring suddenly as they flew over then dying away as they went toward Sainte Maxime.

David and Marita swam back in to the beach and sat on the sand by Catherine.

"They never even looked at me," Catherine said. "They must be very serious boys."

"What did you expect? Aerial photography?" David asked her.

Marita had said very little since they had left the hotel and she said nothing to this.

"It was fun when David really did live with me," Catherine said to her. "I can remember when I liked everything that David did. You must try to like his things too, Heiress. That is if he has any left."

"Do you have any left, David?" Marita asked.

"He traded everything he had in on those stories," Catherine said. "He used to have so many things. I certainly hope you like stories, Heiress."

"I like them," Marita said. She did not look at David but he saw her serene dark face and sea wet hair and smooth lovely skin and her beautiful body as she sat looking out at the sea.

"That's good," Catherine said lazily and took a long deep lazy breath as she stretched out on the beach robe on the sand that was still warm from the afternoon sun. "Because that's what you're going to get. He used to do so many things too and he did them all so beautifully. He had a wonderful life and all he thinks about now is Africa and his drunken father and his press cuttings. His clippings. Has he ever shown you his clippings, Heiress?"

"No, Catherine," Marita said.

"He will," Catherine said. "He tried to show them to me once at le Grau du Roi but I put a stop to that. There were hundreds of them and every one, almost, had his picture and they were all the same pictures. It's worse than carrying around obscene postcards really. I think he reads them by himself and is unfaithful to me with them. In a wastebasket probably. He always has a wastebasket. He said himself it was the most important thing for a writer—"

"Let's go in and swim, Catherine," Marita said. "I think I'm getting cold."

"I mean the wastebasket was the most important thing for a writer," Catherine said. "I used to think I ought to get him a really wonderful one that would be worthy of him. But he never puts anything he writes in the wastebasket. He writes in those ridiculous child's notebooks and he doesn't throw anything away. He just crosses things out and writes along the sides of the pages. The whole business is a fraud really. He makes mistakes in spelling and grammar too. Did you know, Marita, that he doesn't even really know grammar?"

"Poor David," Marita said.

"Of course his French is worse," Catherine said. "You've never seen him try to write it. He fakes along well enough in conversation and he's amusing with his slang. But actually he's illiterate."

"Too bad," said David.

"I thought he was wonderful," Catherine said, "until I found he couldn't write even a simple note correctly. But then you'll be able to write in French for him."

"*Ta gueule*," David said cheerfully.

"He's good at that sort of thing," Catherine said. "Quick tags of slang that are probably outdated before he knows it. He speaks very idiomatic French but he can't write it at all. He's really illiterate, Marita, and you have to face it. His handwriting is terrible too. He can't write like a gentleman nor speak like one in any language. Especially not his own."

"Poor David," Marita said.

"I can't say I've given him the best years of my life," Catherine said. "Because I've only lived with him since March I think it was, but I've certainly given him the best months of my life. The ones I've had the most fun in anyway and he certainly made them fun too. I wish it hadn't ended in complete disillusion too but what are you to do if you discover the man is illiterate and practices solitary vice in a wastebasket full of clippings from something called The Original Romeike's, whoever they are. Any girl would be discouraged and frankly I'm not going to put up with it."

"You take the clippings and burn them," David said. "That would be the soundest thing. Wouldn't you like to go in now and swim, Devil?"

Catherine looked at him slyly.

"How did you know I did it?" she asked.

"Did what?"

"Burned the clippings."

"Did you, Catherine?" Marita asked.

"Of course I did," Catherine said.

David stood looking at her. He felt completely hollow. It was like coming around a curve on a mountain road and the road not being there and only a gulf ahead. Marita was standing now too. Catherine was looking at them her face calm and reasonable.

"Let's go in and swim," Marita said. "We'll just swim out to the point and back."

"I'm glad you're being pleasant finally," Catherine said. "I've been wanting to go in for a long time. It's really getting quite cool. We forget it's September."

Chapter Twenty-six

THEY DRESSED ON THE BEACH and climbed up the steep trail with David carrying the bag with the beach things to where the old car was waiting in the pine woods. They got in and David drove back to the hotel in the early evening light. Catherine was quiet in the car and to anyone passing them they might have been returning from any afternoon at one of the unfrequented beaches of the Estérel. The war ships were no longer in sight when they left the car on the driveway, and the sea beyond the pines was blue and calm. The evening was as beautiful and clear as the morning had been.

They walked down to the entrance of the hotel and David took the bag with the beach things into the storeroom and put it down.

"Let me take them," Catherine said. "They ought to go to dry."

"I'm sorry," David said. He turned at the door of the storeroom and walked out and then down to his work room at the end of the hotel. Inside the room he opened the big Vuitton suitcase. The pile of cahiers that the stories had been written in was gone. So were the four bulky envelopes from the bank that had contained the press clippings. The pile of cahiers with the narrative written in them were intact. He closed and locked the suitcase and searched all of the drawers in the armoire and searched the room. He had not believed that the stories could be gone. He had not believed that she could do it. At the beach he had known that she might have done it but it had seemed impossible and he had not really believed it. They had been calm and careful and restrained about it as you were trained to be in danger or emergency or in disaster but it had not seemed possible that it could really have happened.

Now he knew that it had happened but still thought it might be some ghastly joke. So, empty and dead in his heart, he reopened the suitcase and checked it and after he locked it he checked the room again.

Now there was no danger and no emergency. It was only disaster now. But it couldn't be. She must have hidden them someplace. They could be in the storeroom, or in their own room, or she could have put them in Marita's room. She couldn't really have destroyed them. No one could do that to a fellow human being. He still could not believe that she had done it but he felt sick inside himself when he closed and locked the door.

The two girls were at the bar when David came in. Marita looked up at him and saw how things were and Catherine watched him come in by looking at the mirror. She did not look at him, only at his reflection in the mirror.

"Where did you put them, Devil?" David asked.

She turned away from the mirror and looked at him. "I won't tell you," she said. "I took care of them."

"I wish you'd tell me," David said. "Because I need them very much."

"No, you don't," she said. "They were worthless and I hated them."

"Not the one about Kibo," David said. "You loved Kibo. Don't you remember?"

"He had to go too. I was going to tear him out and keep him but I couldn't find him. Anyway you said he was dead."

David saw Marita look at her and look away. Then she looked back. "Where did you burn them, Catherine?"

"I won't tell you either," Catherine said. "You're part of the same thing."

"Did you burn them with the clippings?" David asked.

"I won't tell you," Catherine said. "You talk to me like a policeman or at school."

"Tell me, Devil. I only want to know."

"I paid for them," Catherine said. "I paid the money to do them."

"I know," David said. "It was very generous of you. Where did you burn them, Devil?"

"I won't tell her."

"No. Just tell me."

"Ask her to go away."

"I really have to go anyway," Marita said. "I'll see you later, Catherine."

"That's good," Catherine said. "It wasn't your fault, Heiress."

David sat on the tall stool by Catherine and she looked in the mirror and watched Marita go out of the room.

"Where did you burn them, Devil?" David asked. "You can tell me now."

"She wouldn't understand," Catherine said. "That's why I wanted her to go."

"I know," said David. "Where did you burn them, Devil?"

"In the iron drum with holes that Madame uses to burn trash," Catherine said.

"Did everything burn up?"

"Yes. I poured on some petrol from a *bidon* in the *remise*. It made a big fire and everything burned. I did it for you, David, and for all of us."

"I'm sure you did," David said. "Did everything burn?"

"Oh yes. We can go out and look if you like but it isn't necessary. The paper all burned black and I stirred it up with a stick."

"I'll just go out and have a look," David said.

"But you'll be back," Catherine said.

"Sure," David said.

The burning had been in the trash burner which was a former fifty-five-gallon gasoline drum with holes punched in it. The stick used to stir the ashes, and still freshly blackened on one end, was an old broom handle which had been used in this capacity before. The *bidon* was in the stone shed and contained kerosene. In the drum were a few identifiable charred bits of the green covers of the cahiers, and David found scraps of burnt newsprint and two charred bits of pink paper which he identified as those used by the Romeike's clipping service. On one he could distinguish the Providence RI dateline. The ashes had been well stirred but there would doubtless have been more unburned or charred material if he had cared to sift or examine them patiently. He tore the pink paper with Providence RI printed on it into small pieces and dropped them in the former gasoline drum which he had replaced in an upright position. He reflected that he had never been in Providence, Rhode Island, and replacing the broom handle in the stone shed, where he noticed the presence of his racing bicycle, the tires of which needed inflation, he reentered the kitchen of the hotel, which was empty, and proceeded to the salon where he joined his wife Catherine at the bar.

"Wasn't it just the way I said?" Catherine asked.

"Yes," David said and sat down on one of the stools and put his elbows on the bar.

"It probably would have been enough to burn the clippings,"

Catherine said. "But I really thought I ought to make a clean sweep."

"You did, all right," David said.

"Now you can go right on with the narrative and there will be nothing to interrupt you. You can start in the morning."

"Sure," David said.

"I'm glad you're reasonable about it," Catherine said. "You couldn't know how worthless they were, David. I had to show you."

"You couldn't have kept the Kibo one that you liked?"

"I told you I tried to find it. But if you want to rewrite it I can tell it to you word for word."

"That will be fun."

"It will be really. You'll see. Do you want me to tell it to you now? We could if you want."

"No," David said. "Not just now. Would you write it though?"

"I can't write things, David. You know that. But I can tell it to you anytime you want. You don't really care about the others do you? They were worthless."

"Why did you do it really?"

"To help you. You can go to Africa and write them again when your viewpoint is more mature. The country can't be changed very much. I think it would be nice if you wrote about Spain instead though. You said the country was almost the same as Africa and there you'd have the advantage of a civilized language."

David poured himself a whiskey and found a bottle of Perrier, uncapped it and poured some in the glass. He remembered the day they had passed the place where they bottled Perrier water on the plain on the way to Aigues Mortes and how—"Let's not talk about writing," he said to Catherine.

"I like to," Catherine said. "When it's constructive and has some valid purpose. You always wrote so well until you started those stories. The worst thing was the dirt and the flies and the cruelty and the bestiality. You seemed almost to grovel in it. That horrible one about the massacre in the crater and the heartlessness of your own father."

"Can we not talk about them?" David asked.

"I want to talk about them," Catherine said. "I want to make you realize why it was necessary to burn them."

"Write it out," David said. "I'd rather not hear it now."

"But I can't write things, David."

"You will," David said.

"No. But I'll tell them to someone who can write them," Catherine said. "If you were friendly you'd write them for me. If you really loved me you'd be happy to."

"All I want to do is kill you," David said. "And the only reason I don't do it is because you are crazy."

"You can't talk to me like that, David."

"No?"

"No, you can't. You can't. Do you hear me?"

"I hear you."

"Then hear me say you can't say such things. You can't say horrible things like that to me."

"I hear you," David said.

"You can't say such things. I won't stand for it. I'll divorce you."

"That would be very welcome."

"Then I'll stay married to you and never give you a divorce."

"That would be pretty."

"I'll do anything I want to you."

"You have."

"I'll kill you."

"I wouldn't give a shit," David said.

"You can't even talk like a gentleman at a time like this."

"What would a gentleman say at a time like this?"

"That he was sorry."

"All right," David said. "I'm sorry. I'm sorry I ever met you. I'm sorry I ever married you—"

"So am I."

"Shut up please. You can tell it to somebody who can write it down. I'm sorry your mother ever met your father and that they ever made you. I'm sorry you were born and that you grew up. I'm sorry for everything we ever did good or bad—"

"You're not."

"No," he said. "I'll shut up. I didn't mean to make a speech."

"You're just really sorry for yourself."

"Possibly," David said. "But shit, Devil, why did you have to burn them? The stories?"

"I had to, David," she said. "I'm sorry if you don't understand."

He had understood really before he had asked her the question and the question had been, he realized, a rhetorical one. He disliked rhetoric and distrusted those who used it and he was ashamed to have fallen into it. He drank the whiskey and Perrier slowly while he thought how untrue it was that everything that was understood was forgiven and he tightened his own discipline as conscientiously as he would have worked in the old days with the mechanic and the armorer going over the plane, the engine and his guns. It was not necessary then because they did the work perfectly but it was one way of not thinking, and it was, to use a wet word, comforting. Now it *was* necessary because what he had said to Catherine about killing her he had said quite truly and not rhetorically. He was ashamed of the speech which had followed the statement. But there was nothing he could do about the statement which was truly made except tighten his discipline so that he would have it in case he began to lose control. He poured himself another whiskey and put in Perrier again and watched the small bubbles form and break. God damn her to hell, he thought.

"I'm sorry to be stuffy," he said. "I understand of course."

"I'm so glad, David," she said. "I'm going away in the morning."

"Where?"

"To Hendaye and then to Paris to see about artists for the book."

"Really?"

"Yes. I think I should. We've wasted time as it is and today I made so much progress that I just need to keep on."

"How are you going?"

"With the Bug."

"You shouldn't drive alone."

"I want to."

"You shouldn't, Devil. Really. I couldn't let you."

"Can I go on the train? There's one to Bayonne. I can rent a car there or in Biarritz."

"Can we talk about it in the morning?"

"I want to talk about it now."

"You shouldn't go, Devil."

"I'm going," she said. "You're not going to stop me."

"I'm only thinking about the best way."

"No, you're not. You're trying to stop me."

"If you wait we'll go together."

"I don't want to go together. I want to go tomorrow and in the Bug. If you don't agree I'll go by train. You can't stop anyone from going on the train. I'm of age and because I'm married to you doesn't make me your slave or your chattel. I'm going and you can't stop me."

"Will you be coming back?"

"I plan to."

"I see."

"You don't see but it doesn't make any difference. This is a reasoned and coordinated project. These things aren't just tossed off—"

"Into a wastebasket," David said and remembered the discipline and sipped the whiskey and Perrier.

"Are you going to see your lawyers in Paris?" he asked.

"If I have any business with them. I usually see my lawyers. Just because you don't have any lawyers doesn't mean everyone else doesn't have to see their lawyers. Do you want my lawyers to do anything for you?"

"No," David said. "Fuck your lawyers."

"Do you have plenty of money?"

"I'm quite all right on money."

"Really, David? Weren't the stories worth a lot? It's bothered me terribly and I know my responsibility. I'll find out and do exactly what I should."

"You'll what?"

"Do exactly what I should."

"Just what is it you propose to do?"

"I'll have their value determined and I'll have twice that paid into your bank."

"Sounds very generous," David said. "You were always generous."

"I want to be just, David, and it's possible that they were worth, financially, much more than they would be appraised at."

"Who appraises these things?"

"There must be people who do. There are people who appraise everything."

"What sort of people?"

"I wouldn't know, David. But I can imagine such people as the editor of the *Atlantic Monthly*, *Harper's*, *La Nouvelle Revue Française*."

"I'm going out for a while," David said. "Do you feel all right?"

"Except for the fact that I feel I've probably done a great wrong to you that I must try to set right I feel very well," Catherine said. "That was one reason I was going to Paris. I didn't want to tell you."

"Let's not discuss casualties," David said. "So you want to go on the train?"

"No. I want to go in the Bug."

"All right. Go in the Bug. Just drive carefully and don't pass on hills."

"I'll drive the way you taught me and I'll pretend you're with me all the time and talk to you and tell us stories and make up stories about how I saved your life. I always make those up. And with you it will all seem so much shorter and effortless and the speed won't seem fast. I'm going to have fun."

"Good," said David. "Take it as easy as you can. Sleep at Nîmes the first night unless you get off early. They know us at the Imperator."

"I thought I'd get to Carcassonne."

"No, Devil, please."

"Perhaps I can get off early and make Carcassonne. I'd go by Arles and Montpellier and not lose time by Nîmes."

"If you get off late stop at Nîmes."

"It seems so babyish," she said.

"I'll drive with you," he said. "I should."

"No, please. It's important that I do this by myself. It really is. I wouldn't have you."

"All right," he said. "But I ought to go."

"Please don't. You must have confidence in me, David. I'll drive carefully and I'll drive it right straight through."

"You couldn't, Devil. It gets dark early now."

"You mustn't worry. You're sweet to let me go," Catherine said. "But you always did. If I did anything I shouldn't I hope you can forgive me. I'll miss you terribly. I miss you already. Next time we'll drive it together."

"You've had a very busy day," David said. "You're tired. At least let me run your Bugatti down to town and back and give it a check."

He stopped at Marita's door and said, "Do you want to go for a ride?"

"Yes," she said.

"Come on then," he told her.

Chapter Twenty-seven

DAVID GOT INTO THE CAR and Marita climbed in beside him and
he put the car at a stretch of road where the sand drifted across
from the beach and then throttled back and held it in, watching
the papyrus grass ahead on his left and the empty beach and the
sea on his right as he saw the black road ahead. He put the car
at the road again until he saw the white painted bridge coming
at him fast then held his speed as he calculated the distance,
raised his foot from the throttle and pumped the brakes gently.
She was steady and lost momentum at each pump with no devi-
ation and no binding. He brought the car to a stop before the
bridge, downshifted and then put her at the road again in a rising disciplined snarl along the N.6 to Cannes.

"She burned them all," he said.

"Oh David," Marita said and they drove on into Cannes
where the lights were on now and David stopped the car under
the trees in front of the cafe where they had first met.

"Wouldn't you rather go somewhere else?" Marita asked.

"I don't care," David said. "It doesn't make a hell of a lot of difference."

"If you'd rather just drive," Marita offered.

"No. I'd rather cool out," David said. "I just wanted to see if the car was in shape for her to drive it."

"She's going?"

"She says so."

They were sitting at the table on the terrace in the dappled shadow of the leaves of the trees. The waiter had brought Marita a Tio Pepe and David a whiskey and Perrier.

"Do you want me to go with her?" Marita said.

"You don't really think anything will happen to her?"

"No, David. I think she's done her damage for a while."

"Could be," David said. "She burned every fucking thing except the narrative. The stuff about her."

"It's a wonderful narrative," Marita said.

"Don't buck me up," David said. "I wrote it and I wrote what she burned. Don't give me the stuff they feed the troops."

"You can write them again."

"No," David told her. "When it's right you can't remember. Every time you read it again it comes as a great and unbelievable surprise. You can't believe you did it. When it's once right you never can do it again. You only do it once for each thing. And you're only allowed so many in your life."

"So many what?"

"So many good ones."

"But you can remember them. You must."

"Not me and not you and not anybody. They're gone. Once I get them right they're gone."

"She was wicked to you."

"No," David said.

"What then?"

"Hurried," David said. "Everything today was because she was hurried really."

"I hope you'll be as kind to me."

"You just stay around and help me not to kill her. You know what she's going to do don't you? She's going to pay me for the stories so that I won't lose anything."

"No."

"Yes she is. She's going to have her lawyers have them appraised in some fantastic Rube Goldberg manner and then she's going to pay me double the appraisal price."

"Truly, David, she didn't say that."

"She said it and it's infinitely sound. Only the details need working out and what's more the doubling of the appraisal or whatever makes it generous and gives her pleasure."

"You can't let her drive alone, David."

"I know it."

"What are you going to do?"

"I don't know. But let's sit here for a little while," David said. "There isn't any hurry now. I think she's probably tired and gone to sleep. I'd like to go to sleep too, with you, and wake up and find the stuff all there and not gone and go to work again."

"We will sleep and someday when you wake up you'll work as wonderfully as you did this morning."

"You're awfully good," David said. "But you certainly got into a fine lot of trouble when you came in here that night, didn't you?"

"Don't try to put me outside," Marita said. "I know what I got into."

"Sure," said David. "We both know. Do you want another drink?"

"If you do," Marita said and then, "I didn't know it was a battle when I came."

"Neither did I."

"With you it's really only you against time."

"Not the time that's Catherine's."

"Only because her time is different. She's panicked by it. You said tonight that all of today was only hurry. That wasn't true but it was perceptive. And you won so well over time for so long."

Very much later he called for the waiter and paid for the drinks and left a good tip and he had started the car and put on the lights and was letting out the clutch when what had really happened came back to him again. It was back as clear and unblurred as when he had first looked into the trash burner and seen the ashes that had been stirred by the broomstick. He pushed his headlights carefully out through the quiet and empty evening of the town and followed them along the port onto the road. He felt Marita's shoulder by him and heard her say, "I know, David. It hit me too."

"Don't let it."

"I'm glad it did. There's nothing to do but we'll do it."

"Good."

"We'll really do it. *Toi et moi.*"

Chapter Twenty-eight

AT THE HOTEL Madame came in from the kitchen when David and Marita came into the main room. She had a letter in her hand.

"Madame took the train for Biarritz," she said. "She left this letter for Monsieur."

"When did she go?" David asked.

"Immediately after Monsieur and Madame left," Madame Aurol said. "She sent the boy to the station for the ticket and to reserve a *wagon-lit.*"

David began reading the letter.

"What would you eat?" Madame said. "Some cold chicken and a salad? An omelette to start. There's lamb too if Monsieur would rather. What would he like, Madame?"

Marita and Madame Aurol were talking together and David finished reading the letter. He put it in his pocket and looked at Madame Aurol. "Did she seem herself when she left?"

"Perhaps not, Monsieur."

"She'll be back," David said.

"Yes, Monsieur."

"We will take good care of her."

"Yes, Monsieur." She began to cry a little as she turned the omelette and David put his arm around her and kissed her. "Go and talk to Madame," she said, "and let me set the table. Aurol and the boy are at Napoule, mixing *belote* and politics."

"I'll set it," Marita said. "Open the wine, David, please. Don't you think we should have a bottle of the Lanson?"

He closed the door of the ice chest and holding the cold bottle untwisted the seal and loosened the wire and then carefully moved the cork between his thumb and first finger feeling the pinch of metal cap against his thumb and the long cold rounded promise of the bottle. He brought the cork out gently and poured three glasses full. Madame stood back from the stove with her glass and they all raised their glasses. David did not know what to drink to so he said the first words that came which were, *"À nous et à la liberté."*

They all drank and then Madame served the omelette and they all drank again without making a toast.

"Eat, David, please," Marita said.

"All right," he said and drank some of the wine and ate some of the omelette slowly.

"Just eat a little," Marita said. "It will be good for you."

Madame looked at Marita and shook her head. "Nothing is helped by your not eating," Madame told him.

"Sure," said David and ate slowly and carefully and drank the champagne that was born new each time he poured a glass.

"Where did she leave the car?" he asked.

"At the station," Madame said. "The boy rode down with her. He brought back the key. It's in your room."

"Was the *wagon-lit* crowded?"

"No. He put her aboard. There were very few passengers. She will have a place."

"It's not a bad train," David said.

"Eat some chicken," Madame said, "and drink some more wine. Open another bottle. Your women are thirsty too."

"I'm not thirsty," Marita said.

"Yes, you are," Madame said. "Drink up now and take a bottle with you. I know this one. It's good for him to drink good wine."

"I don't want to drink too much, *chérie*," David said to Madame. "Because tomorrow is a bad day and I'd rather not feel bad too."

"You won't. I know you. Just eat now to please me."

She excused herself in a few minutes and was gone for a quarter of an hour. David ate all of his chicken and the salad finally and after she had come back they all had a glass of wine together and then David and Marita said good night to Madame who was very formal now and went out onto the terrace and looked at the night. They were both in a hurry and David was carrying the opened bottle of wine in an ice bucket. He put it down on the stove and took Marita in his arms and kissed her. They held each other close and said nothing and then David picked up the bucket and they walked to Marita's room.

Her bed had been made up now for two people and David put the ice bucket down on the floor and said, "Madame."

"Yes," Marita said. "Naturally."

They lay together with the night clear and cool outside and the small breeze from the sea and Marita said, "I love you, David, and it's so sure now."

Sure, David thought. Sure. Nothing is sure.

"All the time before now," Marita said, "before I could sleep all night with you I've thought and thought you wouldn't like the sort of wife who couldn't sleep."

"What sort of wife are you?"

"You'll see. A happy one now."

Then he felt it was a long time before he went to sleep but really it was not and when he woke at the first gray light he saw Marita in the bed beside him and was happy until he remembered what had happened. He was very careful not to wake her but when she stirred he kissed her before he stepped out of bed. She smiled and said, "Good morning, David," and he said, "Go back to sleep my dearest love."

She said, "All right," and rolled over quickly like a small animal and, dark headed, lay curled up with her closed eyes away from the light and her long dark shiny eyelashes against the rose brown early morning color of her skin. David looked at her and thought how beautiful she was and how he could see her spirit had not gone from her body when she slept. She was lovely and her coloring and the unbelievable smoothness of her skin were almost Javanese, he thought. He watched the coloring in her face deepen as the light grew stronger. Then he shook his head and carrying his clothing on his left arm opened and closed the door and went out into the new morning, walking barefoot on the stones that were still wet with dew.

In his and Catherine's room he took a shower, shaved, found a fresh shirt and shorts and put them on, looked around the empty bedroom, the first morning he had ever been in it with Catherine not there, and then went out to the empty kitchen and found a tin of Maquereau Vin Blanc Capitaine Cook and opened it and took it, perilous with edge-level juice, with a cold bottle of the Tuborg beer out to the bar.

He opened the beer, took the bottle top between his right thumb and the first joint of his right forefinger and bent it in until it was flattened together, put it in his pocket since he saw no container to toss it into, raised the bottle that was still cold to his hand and now beaded wet in his fingers and, smelling the aroma from the opened tin of spiced and marinated mackerel, he took a long drink of the cold beer, set it down on the bar and took an envelope from his hip pocket and unfolded Catherine's letter and commenced to reread it.

David, I knew very suddenly you must know how terrible it was. Worse than hitting someone, a child is the worst I guess—with a car. The thump on the fender or maybe just a small bump and then all the rest of it happening and the crowd gathering to scream. The Frenchwoman screaming *écrasseuse* even if it was the child's fault. I did it and I knew I did it and I can't undo it. It's too awful to understand. But it happened.

I'll cut this short. I'll be back and we'll settle things the best we can. Do not worry at all. I'll wire and write and do all the things for my book so if you ever finish it only I will try to do this one thing. I had to burn the other things. The worst was being righteous about it but I don't have to tell you that. I do not ask for forgiveness but please have good luck and I will do everything as well as I can.

Heiress has been good to you and me both and I don't hate her.

I won't end as I'd like to because it would sound too preposterous to believe but I will say it anyway since I was always rude and presumptuous and preposterous too lately as we both know. I love you and I always will and I am sorry. What a useless word.

Catherine

After he had finished it he read it through again.

He had never read any other letters from Catherine because from the time they had met at the Crillon bar in Paris until they were married at the American church at Avenue Hoche they had seen each other every day and, reading this first one now for the third time, he found that he still could be, and was, moved by her.

He put the letter back in his hip pocket and ate a second small, plump, miniature mackerel in the aromatic white wine sauce and finished the cold beer. Then he went out to the kitchen for a piece of bread to sop up the liquid in the long tin and for a fresh bottle of beer. He would try to work today and would almost certainly fail. There had been too much emotion, too much damage, too much of everything and his changing of allegiance, no matter how sound it had seemed, no matter how it simplified things for him, was a grave and violent thing and this letter compounded the gravity and the violence.

All right Bourne, he thought as he began to drink the second beer, don't spend time thinking how bad things are because you know. You have three choices. Try to remember one that is gone and write it again. Second, you can try a new one. And third, write on the god damned narrative. So sharpen up and take the best one. You always gambled when you could bet on yourself. Never bet on anything that can talk, your father said and you said, Except yourself. And he said, Not me, Davey, but pile it on yourself sometime you iron-hearted little bastard. He meant to say cold-hearted but he turned it kindly with his gently lying mouth. Or maybe he meant it. Don't con yourself on Tuborg beer.

So take the best one and write one new and good as you can. And remember, Marita has been hit as badly as you. Maybe worse. So gamble. She cares as much for what we lost as you do.

Chapter Twenty-nine

WHEN HE FINALLY gave up writing that day it was afternoon. He had started a sentence as soon as he had gone into his working room and had completed it but he could write nothing after it. He crossed it out and started another sentence and again came to the complete blankness. He was unable to write the sentence that should follow although he knew it. He wrote a first simple declarative sentence again and it was impossible for him to put down the next sentence on paper. At the end of two hours it was the same. He could not write more than a single sentence and the sentences themselves were increasingly simple and completely dull. He kept at it for four hours before he knew that resolution was powerless against what had happened. He admitted it without accepting it, closed and put away the notebook with the rows of crossed out lines and went to find the girl.

She was on the terrace in the sun reading and when she looked up and saw his face she said, "No?"

"Worse than no."

"Not at all?"

"Nope."

"Let's have a drink," Marita said.

"Good," said David.

They were inside at the bar and the day had come in with them. It was as good as the day before and perhaps better since summer should have been gone and each warm day was an extra thing. We should not waste it, David thought. We should try to make it good and save it if we can. He mixed the martinis and poured them and when they tasted them they were icy cold and dry.

"You were right to try this morning," Marita said. "But let's not think about it any more today."

"Good," he said.

He reached for the bottle of Gordon's, the Noilly Prat and the stirring pitcher, poured out the water from the ice, and using his empty glass commenced to measure out two more drinks.

"It's a lovely day," he said. "What should we do?"

"Let's go to swim now," Marita said. "So we won't waste the day."

"Good," David said. "Should I tell Madame that we'll be late for lunch?"

"She put a cold lunch up," Marita said. "I thought that probably you'd like to swim however work went."

"That was intelligent," David said. "How is Madame?"

"She has a slightly discolored eye," Marita said.

"No."

Marita laughed.

They drove up the road and around the promontory through the forest and left the car in the broken shade of the pine woods and carried the lunch basket and the beach gear down the trail to the cove. There was a little breeze from the east and the sea was dark and blue as they came down through the stone pines. The rocks were red and the sand of the cove was yellow and wrinkled and the water, as they came to it, clean and now amber clear over the sand. They put the basket and the rucksack in the

All right."

They swam far out, further than they had ever swum before, enough so they could see past the next headland and on out until they could see the broken purple line of the mountains behind the forest. They lay there in the water and watched the coast. Then they swam in slowly. They stopped to rest when they lost the mountains and again when they lost the headland and then swam slowly and strongly on in past the entrance to the cove and pulled themselves out on the beach.

"Are you tired?" David asked.

"Very," Marita said. She had never swum that far before.

"Are you still pounding?"

"Oh I'm fine."

David walked up the beach and over to the rock and found one of the bottles of Tavel and two towels.

"You look like a seal," David said sitting down beside her on the sand.

He handed her the Tavel and she drank from the bottle and handed it back. He took a long drink and then on the smooth dry sand, stretched out in the sun, the lunch basket by them and the wine cool as they drank from the bottle. Marita said, "Catherine wouldn't have gotten tired."

"The hell she wouldn't. She never swam that far."

"Truly?"

"We swam a long way, girl. I was never out where we could see those backdrop mountains before."

"All right," she said. "There isn't anything we can do about her today so let's not think about it. David?"

"Yes."

"Do you still love me?"

"Yes. Very much."

"Perhaps I made a great mistake with you and you're just being kind to me."

"You didn't make any mistakes and I'm not being kind to you."

shade of the biggest rock and undressed and Da
tall rock to dive. He stood there naked and bro
looking out to the sea.

"Want to dive?" he called.

She shook her head.

"I'll wait for you."

"No," she called up and waded out into the water
thighs.

"How is it?" David called down.

"Much cooler than it's ever been. Almost cold."

"Good," he said, and as she watched him and waded, t
ter came over her belly and touched her breasts and he str
ened, rose on his toes, seemed to hang slowly without fa
and then knifed out and down, making a boil in the water th
porpoise might have made reentering slickly into the hole t
he had made in rising. She swam out toward the circle of milli
water and then he rose beside her and held her up and close an
then put his salty mouth against her own.

"*Elle est bonne, la mer,*" he said. "*Toi aussi.*"

They swam out of the cove and beyond into the deep water
past where the mountain dropped down into the sea, and lay on
their backs and floated. The water was colder than it had been
but the very top was warmed a little and Marita floated with her
back arched high, her head all underwater but her nose, and her
brown breasts were lapped gently by the movement the light
breeze gave the sea. Her eyes were shut against the sun and
David was beside her in the water. His arm was under her head
and then he kissed the tip of her left breast and then the other
breast.

"They taste like the sea," he said.

"Let's go to sleep out here."

"Could you?"

"It's too hard to keep my back arched."

"Let's swim way out and then swim in."

Marita took a handful of radishes and ate them slowly and drank some wine. The radishes were young and crisp and sharp in flavor.

"You don't have to worry about working," she said. "I know. That will be all right."

"Sure," David said.

He cut one of the artichoke hearts up with the fork and ate a chunk swirled in the mustard sauce Madame had made.

"May I have the Tavel?" Marita said. She took a good swallow of the wine and set the bottle down by David putting its base firmly in the sand and leaning it against the basket. "Isn't it a good lunch Madame made, David?"

"It's an excellent lunch. Did Aurol really give her a black eye?"

"Not a real one."

"She has a bad tongue with him."

"There's the difference in age and he was within his rights to hit her if she was insulting. She said so. At the end. And she sent you messages."

"What messages?"

"Just loving messages."

"She loves *you*," David said.

"No. You stupid. She's only on my side."

"There aren't any sides anymore," David said.

"No," Marita said. "And we didn't try to make sides. It just happened."

"It happened all right." David handed her the jar with the cut up artichoke heart and the dressing and found the second bottle of Tavel. It was still cool. He took a long drink of the wine. "We've been burned out," he said. "Crazy woman burned out the Bournes."

"Are we the Bournes?"

"Sure. We're the Bournes. It may take a while to have the papers. But that's what we are. Do you want me to write it out? I think I could write that."

"You don't need to write it."

"I'll write it in the sand," David said.

They slept well and naturally through the late afternoon and when the sun was low Marita woke and saw David lying in the bed by her side. His lips were closed and he was breathing very slowly and she looked at his face and his covered eyes that she had only seen lidded in sleep twice before and looked at his chest and his body with the arms straight by his sides. She went over to the door of the bathroom and looked at herself in the full length mirror. Then she smiled at the mirror. When she was dressed she went out to the kitchen and talked with Madame.

Later, David was still asleep and she sat by him on the bed. In the dusk his hair was whitish against his dark face, and she waited for him to wake.

They sat at the bar and were both drinking Haig Pinch and Perrier. Marita was being very careful with her drink. She said, "I think you should go to town every day and get the papers and have a drink and read by yourself. I wish there was a club or a real cafe where you met your friends."

"There isn't."

"Well, I think it would be good every day for you to be away from me for a while when you're not working. You've been over-run with girls. I'm always going to see you have your men friends. That's one thing very bad that Catherine did."

"Not on purpose and it was my own fault."

"Maybe that's true. But do you think we'll have friends? Good friends?"

"We each have one already."

"Will we have others?"

"Maybe."

"Will they take you away because they know more than I do?"

"They won't know more."

"Will they come along young and new and fresh with new things and you be tired of me?"

"They won't and I won't be."

"I'll kill them if they do. I'm not going to give you away to anyone the way she did."

"That's good."

"I want you to have men friends and friends from the war and to shoot with and to play cards at the club. But we don't have to have you have women friends, do we? Fresh, new ones who will fall in love and really understand you and all that?"

"I don't run around with women. You know that."

"They are new all the time," Marita said. "There are new ones every day. No one can ever be sufficiently warned. You most of all."

"I love you," David said, "and you're my partner too. But take it easy. Just be with me."

"I'm with you."

"I know it and I love to look at you and know you're here and that we'll sleep together and be happy."

In the dark, Marita lay against him and he felt her breasts against his chest and her arm behind his head and her hand touching him and lips against his.

"I'm your girl," she said in the dark. "Your girl. No matter what I'm always your girl. Your good girl who loves you."

"Yes, my dearest love. Sleep well. Sleep well."

"You go to sleep first," Marita said, "and I'll be back in a minute."

He was asleep when she came back and she got in under the sheet and lay beside him. He was sleeping on his right side and breathing softly and steadily.

Chapter Thirty

DAVID WOKE IN THE MORNING when the first light came in the window. It was still gray outside and there were different pine trunks than the ones he usually woke to see and a longer gap beyond them toward the sea. His right arm was stiff because he had slept on it. Then, awake, he knew he was in a strange bed and he saw Marita lying sleeping by him. He remembered everything and he looked at her lovingly and covered her fresh brown body with the sheet and then kissed her very lightly again and putting on his dressing gown walked out into the dew-wet early morning carrying the image of how she looked with him to his room. He took a cold shower, shaved, put on a shirt and a pair of shorts and walked down to his working room. He stopped at the door of Marita's room and opened it very carefully. He stood and looked at her sleeping, and closed the door softly and went into the room where he worked. He got out his pencils and a new cahier, sharpened five pencils and began to write the story of his father and the raid in the year of the Maji-Maji rebellion that had started with the trek across the bitter lake. He made the crossing now and completed the dreadful trek of the first day when the sunrise had caught them with the part that had to be done in the dark only half finished and the mirages already making as the heat became unbearable. By the time the morning was well advanced and a strong fresh east breeze was blowing through the pines from the sea he had finished the night at the first camp under the fig trees where the water came down from the escarpment and was moving out of that camp in the early morning and up the long draw that led to the steep cut up onto the escarpment.

He found he knew much more about his father than when he had first written this story and he knew he could measure his progress by the small things which made his father more tactile and to have more dimensions than he had in the story before. He was fortunate, just now, that his father was not a simple man.

David wrote steadily and well and the sentences that he had made before came to him complete and entire and he put them down, corrected them, and cut them as if he were going over proof. Not a sentence was missing and there were many that he put down as they were returned to him without changing them. By two o'clock he had recovered, corrected and improved what it had taken him five days to write originally. He wrote on a while longer now and there was no sign that any of it would ever cease returning to him intact.

About the Author

Ernest Hemingway was born in Oak Park, Illinois, in 1899, and began his writing career for *The Kansas City Star* in 1917. During the First World War he volunteered as an ambulance driver on the Italian front but was invalided home, having been seriously wounded while serving with the infantry. In 1921 Hemingway settled in Paris, where he became part of the expatriate circle of Gertrude Stein, F. Scott Fitzgerald, Ezra Pound, and Ford Madox Ford. With the appearance of *The Sun Also Rises* in 1926, Hemingway became not only the voice of the "lost generation" but the preeminent writer of his time. This was followed by his novel of the Italian front, *A Farewell to Arms* (1929). In the 1930s, Hemingway settled in Key West, and later in Cuba, but he traveled widely—to Spain, Italy, and Africa. Later he reported on the Spanish Civil War, which became the background for his brilliant war novel, *For Whom the Bell Tolls* (1939), hunted U-boats in the Caribbean, and covered the European front during the Second World War. Hemingway's most popular work, *The Old Man and the Sea*, was awarded the Pulitzer Prize in 1953, and in 1954 Hemingway won the Nobel Prize in Literature "for his powerful, style-forming mastery of the art of narration." One of the most important influences on the development of the short story and novel in American fiction, Hemingway has seized the imagination of the American public like no other twentieth-century author. He died, by suicide, in Ketchum, Idaho, in 1961. His other major works include *To Have and Have Not* (1937), *Across the River and Into the Trees* (1950), and posthumously, *A Moveable Feast* (1964), *Islands in the Stream* (1970), *The Dangerous Summer* (1985), and *The Garden of Eden* (1986).